MURDER
AT THE ARTS FESTIVAL

Irish crime fiction at its best

DAVID PEARSON

THE BOOK FOLKS

Paperback edition published by

The Book Folks

London, 2023

This book is a work of fiction. Names, characters, businesses, organizations, places and events are either the product of the author's imagination or are used fictitiously. Any resemblance to actual persons, living or dead, events or locales is entirely coincidental. The spelling is British English.

ISBN 978-1-80462-071-7

www.thebookfolks.com

MURDER AT THE ARTS FESTIVAL is the fourteenth standalone mystery in The Galway Homicides series. Details about the other titles can be found at the back of this book.

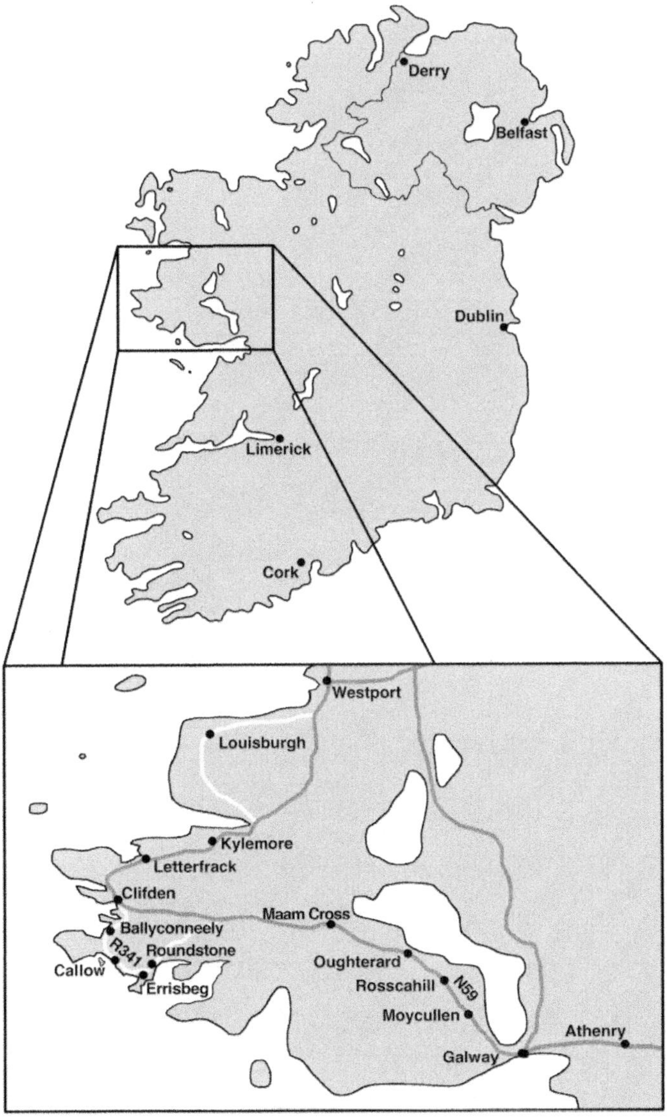
Derry
Belfast
Dublin
Limerick
Cork
Westport
Louisburgh
Kylemore
Letterfrack
Clifden
Maam Cross
Ballyconneely
R341
Roundstone
Callow
Errisbeg
Oughterard
Rosscahill
N59
Moycullen
Athenry
Galway

Chapter One

The Clifden Arts Festival marks the end of the tourist season on the west coast of County Galway. It is a colourful affair, with a candlelit parade through the streets, various exhibits in local venues, and even a studio bus tour to keep all and sundry entertained.

The festival, which runs from mid-September for ten days, claims to be the oldest arts festival in Ireland, and it attracts a very good crowd, keeping the town's hotels and pubs busy in what would otherwise be a quiet month. By this time, most of the holiday cottages and second homes dotted around Connemara are deserted, as the children have returned to school, and their parents to work in the cities.

The festival is centred around The Showgrounds, which is a large field that serves many purposes. A large marquee is erected and artists of all types promote and sell their works during the festival. There are paintings of the locality, displayed by a number of artists, some of which are quite good, others not so; sculpture of various kinds ranging from completely abstract to easily identifiable people or animals; and the inevitable array of scented candles, along with some home-made baking and even a few local cheeses.

For the Gardaí attached to Clifden and Roundstone, the event imposes but a small burden on the force. Parking in the town can be an issue, and very occasionally there is some rowdiness from young people who have imbibed a little too much in the hostelries of Clifden, but generally the festival is a peaceful affair, and the local police adopt quite a tolerant approach, providing more friendly advice than harsh enforcement.

But this year, when the festival was in full swing, things changed.

It was just after half past eight in the morning when Charlie Gifford left his home and walked the ten minutes or thereabouts down through the town to the showgrounds. It would be a busy day. At one end of the marquee, trestle tables would be laden with home-made cakes, biscuits, scones and the like, along with a huge urn full of tea to provide sustenance for the many visitors that were expected.

Charlie was a sort of unofficial groundsman for the festival. A retired gentleman in his late sixties, he had run a small drapers shop in Clifden for many years, selling hand-knitted Aran sweaters and other locally produced woollen goods, as well as ready-made suits and outerwear, so much in demand for the fickle weather that was often encountered in the area. When he retired, he passed the business to his daughter, Aoife, who overhauled the shop and the stock on offer, and was now doing rather well catering for the younger folk in Clifden with more contemporary clothing and a less fusty style of customer service. Gone was the long, mahogany counter behind which there had been drawers and boxes holding volumes of mostly outdated goods. The shop had been opened up and was now brightly lit and inviting, and while her father didn't entirely approve of the modifications, he had to admit that turnover had increased dramatically, and profits too.

Charlie arrived at the gates to the showgrounds and unlocked the stout padlock that was securing the premises, unwinding the shiny new chain that had been procured especially for the event, and leaving it in a small metal box behind the gates themselves. He walked across the damp grass towards the marquee, cursing to himself that he hadn't put on his wellington boots, as his brown leather town shoes were getting soaked.

When he got to the large white tent, he rolled back the flap that was used as an entrance and tied it off. The air inside the marquee smelled of warm canvas, but there was another whiff altogether that didn't sit right in Charlie Gifford's nostrils. He followed the smell across the plywood floor to where the trestle tables stood lined up at right angles to the entrance, covered in white plastic tablecloths. Gifford, by now getting a sense that something was amiss, walked behind the row of tables, and immediately recoiled in horror. For there, lying at an awkward angle on the floor, was a fully clothed man staring lifelessly up at the roof of the marquee.

Gifford realised that the man was dead, and that realisation seemed to paralyse his brain, so that for a few moments, he couldn't process what he had encountered, nor what to do about it. He put his right hand, palm down, on the nearest table to steady himself. After a few moments, his faculties began to clear, and although he was still rooted to the spot, he knew that he had to call for assistance.

He reached into the side pocket of his cavalry twill trousers and took out his Nokia push-button phone. Making some considerable effort to focus on the device, he pressed the '9' three times and lifted the phone to his ear.

"Emergency. Which service do you require, caller?" the call handler at the Ballyshannon Emergency Call Answering Service said.

"Eh, police, please."

The call handler identified the location that the call was coming from, and prepared to direct the call to Clifden.

"May I have your name, please, caller?"

"Eh... Gifford, Charlie Gifford."

"And what is the nature of your emergency, Mr Gifford?"

"I've found a body. A dead body. At least I'm pretty certain he's dead. It's here at the showgrounds. Can you get someone to help?"

"I'm putting you through now, Mr Gifford. Do you need an ambulance as well?"

"Eh... I'm not sure, well, yes, I suppose so."

* * *

Sergeant Séan Mulholland was the officer in charge of Clifden Garda station. He normally opened the station at nine o'clock, but while the festival was going on, he made the effort to get the place open a bit earlier so that he could issue instructions to his own uniformed officers and the six extra Gardaí that had been lent to him for the week to assist with the additional workload brought on by the arts festival. But his first action at the station was, as always, to put on the kettle and brew a mug of tea for himself and whoever else was around, and he was pleased to see that there was still about half a pint of milk left in the fridge from yesterday. His catering endeavours were disturbed by the ringing of the station's telephone.

"God dammit. Can a man not get a cup of tea without that bloody thing interrupting?" he said to himself, putting the kettle down, his mug only half full of boiling water.

"Clifden Gardaí," he said a little grumpily.

Charlie Gifford recognised the voice of the sergeant immediately.

"Oh, Sergeant Mulholland, it's Charlie Gifford here. Look, I'm down at the showgrounds. I came in early to open up the place, and I have found a body here in the big tent."

"A body, is it? Good God. Are you sure, Charlie? Maybe he's just sleeping it off. Who is this fella anyway – I presume it is a man?"

"It is of course. But listen, Sergeant, I need you to come down here straight away. I'm not the better of this yet, and people will be arriving soon to set the place up for the day."

"All right, all right. I'll be down directly. For heaven's sake don't touch anything, and keep everyone else away. Has an ambulance been called?"

"Yes, I think so. The call handler said he would get one."

"Right, so. Stay put then, Charlie. I'll be down in a couple of minutes."

As Mulholland put down the phone, his right-hand man Garda Jim Dolan arrived in.

"Morning, Sarge. What's the craic?" Dolan said.

"That was Charlie Gifford on the phone. He reckons he's found a dead body down at the showgrounds. I suppose we'd better go down and take a look. It's probably just some bloke who had a few too many last night and never made it home. But we'd better go and see what's up. Will you phone Peadar and tell him where we are and ask him to look after the place till we get back?"

"Yeah, OK. Will we take the car?" Dolan said.

"Yes, we'd better."

Chapter Two

The two Gardaí drove the short distance to the showgrounds where Charlie Gifford was waiting anxiously at the gates he had opened just a short time previously. Mulholland pulled up the vehicle close to the entrance, and they both got out.

"Good morning, Charlie. What's the story here? Has your dead body come around yet? Must have been good craic last night," Jim Dolan said, smiling. But Gifford wasn't amused.

The trio walked slowly across the lush green turf, now a little churned up from the activity that had taken place over the past few days. They reached the marquee, and Gifford said, "I'll wait here if you don't mind, Sergeant."

"Good idea, Charlie. No point in contaminating the scene, after all, is there?" Mulholland said winking at his colleague who just smiled cynically.

"He's at the back there, behind the tables," Charlie Gifford called after the two Gardaí as they oriented themselves in the large, somewhat airless space.

"Oh, right. Thanks," Mulholland said.

Moving together to the gap between the trestle tables and the side wall of the marquee, now flapping gently in the breeze, Jim Dolan and Séan Mulholland discovered what Charlie Gifford had described.

The man lying on the floor, with a blueish tinge to his face, was probably in his forties. He had a good head of dark brown hair, neatly trimmed, just showing the first signs of greying above his ears. He was dressed in blue denim jeans, a loud check shirt, and a sort of beige knitted jacket with leather patches on the shoulders. The man was not overweight, and his good leather boots hinted at someone who was certainly not poor. He was lying partially on his back, but his left leg, which was mostly underneath him, was twisted at an unlikely angle, and looked extremely uncomfortable.

"Christ, Charlie might have been right all along, Jim. This looks more than just a hangover to me," Mulholland said. "You stand back there so as not to contaminate the scene. I'll check him for a pulse."

Using the nearest table for support, Séan Mulholland leaned in across the body and placed his index and second finger on the side of the man's neck. But there was no vestige of life to be found. He stood up stiffly and said to Dolan, "It's strange, Jim, he looks healthy enough, but he's definitely a goner. Anyway, we'd better call in the cavalry. Will you get a few of the lads down to secure the place – no one in or out except for the usual crowd, and everyone recorded. Get tape up all around this paddock too. I'll get onto Galway."

"Right, Sarge."

"Oh, and have a word with Charlie too. See who's in charge of the festival. We'll have to keep it closed till at least the pathologist gets here, and maybe longer."

"Oh, yes, of course, I'll go and find Charlie now," Dolan said.

* * *

Senior Detective Inspector Maureen Lyons was enjoying a very rare morning off, or so she thought. Her partner, Detective Superintendent Mick Hays had left to go to work in Galway's Garda headquarters in Mill Street at just after eight o'clock, and Lyons was enjoying a long soak in a hot bath with luxurious bubbles all around her.

She didn't initially hear her mobile phone ringing on the bedside table, but when it rang for a second time, the persistent and rather annoying tune caught her attention. She climbed out of the bath, hastily wrapped a robe around her, and dashed for the instrument disturbing her peace.

"Lyons," she said, fumbling with the device, her hands being slippery from soap.

"Good morning, Inspector. It's Danny here from Mill Street. I've just had a call from Sergeant Mulholland out in Clifden. He says he's found a dead body at the showgrounds out there. I asked him if he was sure the person was dead, but he assured me that he was."

"I see. Is there any suggestion that it's a suspicious death? Are there any obvious signs of foul play, Danny?"

"I don't know. To be honest Sergeant Mulholland was a bit distressed. So, I thought I'd call you myself. Inspector Flynn is away over to Loughrea with a suspect for court there."

"It's fine, Danny. Call him back, will you, and tell him I'm on my way. I'll be there in about an hour."

"Yes, OK, Inspector. Thanks, and sorry to disturb you."

"No worries, Danny. Thanks."

Lyons ended the call.

"So much for a morning of self-indulgent pampering, Maureen. Damn! I hope this isn't a bloody wild goose chase!" Lyons said to herself.

Lyons showered herself off and dressed quickly into work clothes – a fresh white blouse and a navy-blue trouser suit with shiny black shoes. She brushed out her shoulder length chestnut-coloured hair, and let it dry naturally. She hadn't time to get the hairdryer going. Ten minutes after taking the call, she was on the road.

As soon as she got clear of the city with her blue lights flashing in the front and back of her Volvo S60, she used the handsfree system in the car to call Séan Mulholland.

"Hi, Séan. It's Maureen. I'm on my way out there. What's the story?"

Mulholland went on to describe the events of the morning to Lyons.

"I see. Have we any idea who the person is, Séan?"

"No, I'm afraid not. I didn't like to interfere with him once I had established that he was actually dead. It's odd, because he looked OK. A bit blue, but at first I thought he might have just been sleeping it off."

"OK. Well, make sure the scene is preserved, Séan, he could just have died of a heart attack or something."

"Yes, I know. But the place was all closed up last night. It was secured, at least that's what Charlie Gifford said. So, how did he get in and what was he doing there?"

"We'll sort it out when I get there, Séan. I won't be long now. I'm just past Recess. Should I go to the station or the showgrounds?" Lyons said.

"Better come to the showgrounds, Maureen. We need a senior officer to attend the scene in case it is suspicious."

"Right. I'll see you shortly."

As she drove on towards Clifden, she wondered what lay ahead. But as she progressed along the well-worn route, the beauty of the landscape through which she was driving put her more at ease. Overhead, small, patchy, fluffy white clouds gently moved across the sky, and the sun broke through often, creating a patchwork of green and brown on the heathland. A few minutes later, she drew her car up in front of the gates that had earlier been opened by Charlie Gifford. She was pleased to see that Mulholland had protected the place by taping the whole area off with blue and white tape, and that he had also posted a uniformed officer at the entrance.

"Good morning, Guard," she said, displaying her warrant card to the young fresh-faced man, who wrote her name on his clipboard and asked her to sign.

Once inside the grounds, she pulled on blue plastic overshoes and walked directly to the large white marquee, drew aside the flap that served as a door, and went in.

"Good morning, Inspector. He's over here," Séan Mulholland said, gesturing to the area behind the trestle table.

"Morning, Séan. Have we any idea who he is yet?" Lyons said.

"No. I thought I'd wait for you to get here," the officer said, clearly relieved to see a senior Garda in attendance.

Lyons donned protective vinyl gloves and approached the supine form of the man on the floor. She studied the scene for a few minutes, before getting down on her hunkers to examine the body more carefully. She patted the man's trouser pockets, and gently searched them, withdrawing a folded white handkerchief gripped between her first two fingers, and a few coins that rolled around on the plywood floor before running off into the grass in the gap between the floor and the tent wall.

"No wallet," she said out loud to no one in particular.

"I'm no expert, but it looks as if rigor has set in, but hasn't gripped the whole body yet. There doesn't seem to be any visible wound on him. Look, Séan, you'd better call Dr Dodd and get him out. I don't like the look of this. Something's not right."

Mulholland didn't reply, but walked towards the door of the tent and called Dr Julian Dodd, the pathologist attached to Galway University Hospital who was well known to the Gardaí. After a few minutes he was back alongside Lyons.

"How did that go?" she asked.

"God, he's a grumpy old fecker at times. But he's on his way – reluctantly. Maybe his humour will have improved by the time he gets here," Mulholland said.

"I wouldn't bank on it!"

Chapter Three

While Lyons and Mulholland were waiting for Dr Julian Dodd to drive out from Galway, they strolled back up the town and went to a small café for refreshments and a snack. The café they had chosen gave them a view of the approach to the showgrounds, so they would be able to see the good doctor arriving.

Mulholland ordered a pot of tea, while Lyons opted for just a cappuccino to which she added two small sachets of sugar.

"Well, Séan, what do you make of this thing then?" Lyons said, stirring the froth into the hot liquid.

"Ah, I dunno, Maureen." The two Gardaí had at one time been of the same rank, so they addressed each other by their first names when there was no one else around.

"It could be something and nothing. But I can't figure out how he got there. The place was closed up yesterday after the festival was over, according to Charlie in any case. And he's fairly good with that sort of thing. Very reliable. And what was the man doing there? There was nothing of value left behind, and he doesn't look like a thief. But there are a good few strangers here in town at the moment, so I guess we'll have to wait till he can be identified at least.

Have you any initial thoughts?" the sergeant said, stirring the rather hot liquid in his teapot vigorously to strengthen the brew. The clanking noise of the spoon against the metal of the pot irritated Maureen Lyons.

"I haven't a clue, Séan. But I know it doesn't feel right. And don't you dare say anything about female intuition," she said, smiling.

"Oh, far be it from me, Maureen. But I agree. There's something fishy. God, I hope we don't have to keep the showgrounds closed for too long. Yer man that runs the thing will go ape."

"Who is actually in charge of this gig anyway, Séan?"

"Mathew Arbuthnot by name. He's an Englishman, and he can be prickly enough, I can tell you. I think he believes we should still all be subjects of the crown, if you know what I mean."

"I do. But I suppose we'd better find him and appraise him of the situation all the same," Lyons said.

"I'll just give Jim Dolan a call and ask him to see to it. Don't worry. You'll be hearing from Arbuthnot soon enough!"

Mulholland made the call to his colleague and asked him to walk up as far as the festival office which was located in three rooms over a chemist's shop on the main street. As he finished the call, Lyons spotted Dr Julian Dodd's sleek and shiny Lexus gliding past the window of the café.

"Here's Dodd," Lyons said to Mulholland, as he had his back to the window. "We'd better go and show him where to go."

Lyons and Mulholland left the café and walked briskly back to the showgrounds. Dr Dodd was at the rear of his car, changing his shiny black leather brogues for a pair of spotlessly clean green wellington boots. The man was nothing if not dapper.

Lyons and Mulholland exchanged a smile as they approached.

"Morning, Doc. Thanks for coming out. I'm not sure what we have here, but no doubt you'll be able to sort it out for us."

Dodd looked up as he pulled the second boot onto his foot.

"Good morning, Inspector, Sergeant. I hope you'll make it worth my while dragging me all the way out here. I have a lunch appointment back in Galway, you know, so I'd like to get on with it."

"Yes, of course. Our man is inside the marquee, and he's dead, I'm afraid," Lyons said.

"I think that's for me to decide, Inspector, don't you? That is what I'm here for, after all."

Lyons and Mulholland exchanged another glance before setting off across the muddy grass towards the big white tent.

Dodd, carrying his well-worn leather Gladstone bag, being small in stature, had to almost trot across the greenery to keep up with his companions. When he had checked in with the man guarding the entrance to the tent, he quickly found his quarry and bent down to examine him.

The doctor, now equipped with strong, black-rimmed glasses, examined the dead man's face, neck and hands. He lifted the man's arm and then placed it back gently at his side. He eased back the man's eyelids, and spent a moment examining the pupils and whites of the eyes, shining a small LED torch into each one in turn. Then he took a little dark plastic strip out of his case, and applied it to the man's slightly clammy forehead.

"Hmm," Dodd said, using the nearby trestle table to assist him getting back to a standing position.

"Well, Doctor, what's the story?" Lyons said.

"I can certify that he is indeed, as you said, deceased. But I imagine in time-honoured fashion you need more information."

"Just the usual, you know: time of death, cause of death, or any other observations."

"I can't give you much till I get him back to town and do the post-mortem. What I can say is that he probably died between 10 p.m. and 3 a.m. this morning. As to what caused it, I can't be sure till we get to see inside him and do some analysis, and as you know, I'm not given to speculation in these matters."

"Is there any sign of him being attacked or mugged?" Lyons said.

"No. In fact there are no visible signs of any blow to the head, or knife wounds for you, Inspector. So, you'll just have to be patient. Shall we say four o'clock this afternoon? I presume transport has been arranged?"

"Yes, they're fairly close behind you along with the forensic folks. Thanks, Doctor."

"Excellent."

Dodd packed away the few bits and pieces that he had used to examine the corpse, removed his blue vinyl gloves and set off back to his car.

As Dodd's vehicle pulled away, the anonymous black Mercedes van drew up at the gates along with the white Toyota 4x4 used by the forensic team lead, Sinéad Loughran, and her team.

Loughran stepped down from the large vehicle and greeted Maureen Lyons whom she knew well from working with the detectives over several years. Lyons was always impressed with Loughran's good humour, no matter how gruesome the scene that she was investigating. They got on very well, and they frequently went for a drink together after work in Galway.

"Hi, Maureen. What's the story here then?"

"Hi, Sinéad. I'm not sure to be honest. We have a dead guy inside the marquee, but no visible signs of any trauma or anything, so it could just be natural causes, but it doesn't feel right to me somehow."

"Ah, I see. Just let me get suited up and then I'll take a look," Loughran said.

As Loughran was pulling the white plastic scene-of-crime one-piece suit over her slim shape, a man strode towards the two of them. He was tall, slim, with a ruddy complexion, and had a determined look on his face.

"What's going on here and who are you?" he said, addressing Maureen Lyons a little more aggressively than she felt was necessary. Lyons held up her warrant card for the man to inspect without saying anything. He fumbled in his inner pocket for a set of spectacles, put them on, and studied the card for a moment.

"I see," he said, "and what appears to be the problem?"

"May I ask who you are, sir, and what you are doing here?" Lyons said, trying not very successfully to suppress her agitation.

"Arbuthnot," came the clipped reply, "I'm in charge of things around here. Now I don't like to repeat myself, miss. What's going on?"

"It's Senior Inspector Lyons, Mr Arbuthnot – not 'miss'. We're investigating what may be a suspicious death here. A body has been found in the marquee. It's a man," Lyons said dryly.

"Well, get out of my way then and let me see. I'll probably know him," Arbuthnot said, attempting to sidestep and enter through the gate that Lyons was standing in front of.

"I'm afraid you can't go in there, Mr Arbuthnot. It may well be a crime scene, and our forensic team are just about to examine the place."

Arbuthnot looked at Lyons as though she were a naughty schoolgirl brought before the headmaster for a telling off.

"I don't think you understand, Ms Lyons. I am in charge of the arts festival, and we need to get this area open to allow the next exhibition to set up their work, and enable the merchants to get ready for opening at twelve o'clock."

"I'm afraid that's out of the question, sir. No one is going near that tent until I say so. If you care to give me your mobile phone number, I'll call you later when, or should I say, if, we have finished."

Arbuthnot stared at Lyons for a few minutes, and she returned the look without blinking.

"Who is your superior officer? I want to speak to him about this."

"Yes, it does happen to be a man in this instance. His name is Detective Superintendent Michael Hays, and if you call Mill Street Garda station in Galway, they may put you through," Lyons said, turning away from the man to talk to Loughran who had been observing the interaction with a certain amount of amusement.

"Can you not give me his mobile phone number, Ms Lyons?"

"No, I can't. And it's Senior Inspector Lyons to you, sir." And this time, she walked away.

"Jesus, Maureen. What a prick! Well done you," Loughran said when they were barely out of earshot of Arbuthnot who was marching away, his face even redder now.

"A sad case, Sinéad. Now let's go and see what traces have been left for us."

* * *

Twenty minutes later, Loughran stood up from where she had been examining the area around the body carefully.

"Well, anything of interest, Sinéad?" asked Lyons, who had been waiting patiently for Loughran to do her work.

"Very little. I did find this little yellow plastic thing wedged down between the floor and the wall of the marquee," she said, holding up a small evidence bag containing a curved strip of bright yellow plastic with a saw-tooth edge along one side.

"What's that?" Lyons asked.

"I'm not sure. It looks like the kind of seal you get around the top of milk containers, but it's the wrong colour. They are usually either red, blue, or green, and it's smaller in any case."

"If you say so. Anyway, it could have got there at any time and not be connected to your man at all. Any sign of a mobile phone?" Lyons said.

"No, 'fraid not," Loughran said.

"Are we OK to move the body now?" Lyons asked.

"Yes, sure. Best to get him back into Galway and let Dodd have a go at him. There is just one thing I noticed though."

"What's that?"

"An odd-looking circular mark that goes around his nose and under his mouth, as if someone had pressed a pint glass into his face or something. It must have been pushed in quite hard, whatever it was, and it was pre-death, that's for sure."

"Any ID anywhere on him?" Lyons asked.

"No, nothing, though we may be able to get something from his clothes at the PM. Do you want to give the lovely Mr Arbuthnot a look at him before they take him away?"

"Yes, why not. Maybe it will put him off his lunch!"

They both laughed out loud.

Lyons looked up the Clifden Arts Festival on her phone and called the number given, asking to speak to Mr Arbuthnot.

"Mr Arbuthnot, it's Detective Senior Inspector Lyons here. We met earlier." She continued before the man had a chance to respond. "You said you might be able to identify our corpse. Well, if you care to come back down here within the next ten minutes, you can have a look at him before we take him off to the city for the post-mortem."

"It's not very convenient just now. I could be there in half an hour or so?" Arbuthnot said.

"No, don't worry about it. He'll be long gone by then. It was just a thought."

"Oh, very well then. I'll come down directly," he snapped, and hung up without another word.

Chapter Four

Lyons and Loughran were standing by the gate waiting for Arbuthnot to arrive when Lyons' phone started ringing. She looked at the screen and saw that it was Mick Hays.

"Hi, Mick. What's up?"

"Hello to you too. Listen, where are you?"

"In Clifden. There's been a body of a man found at the showgrounds and I'm just here with Sinéad waiting for it to be moved to Galway. Why, do you need me?"

"No, nothing like that, but I hear you've been upsetting the natives… again!" Hays said.

"Ah, the lovely Mr Arbuthnot, no doubt. He's a prick, by the way."

"Well, that's as may be, but he's not without a bit of influence, it seems. What's his involvement anyway?"

"Nothing really. He said he might be able to identify the body, so I've asked him to come down and have a look at it. But he runs the show out here – literately. And he wants the place opened up by twelve. In fact, that won't be a problem, but I'm not letting him off the hook that easily," Lyons said.

"OK, whatever. But don't wind him up too much, hun. He could cause trouble."

"Ah, you're no fun, Mick. I'll let Sinéad loose on him if he's not careful. That'll teach him!"

"Oh, gawd. The poor fella. Well, look, I'll see you later then. Will you be back at teatime?" Hays said.

"Yes. I'll be going into Galway for the PM on the poor man. It may not even be suspicious. He could have just had a heart attack, but I have a feeling that it's not that simple."

"Right. Well, give me a call when you're free and we'll meet up in town."

"OK. See ya."

When the call was ended, Lyons could see Arbuthnot marching towards them looking just as agitated as he had done earlier. At the same time, the body of the deceased was arriving at the gate to the paddock on a portable stretcher with wheels, being shepherded by two sombre-looking men in long black overcoats.

"Have you heard from the superintendent, Inspector?" Arbuthnot said when he was just a few feet away from Lyons.

"No. Should I have?" she lied.

Arbuthnot just grunted.

"This is my colleague, Sinéad Loughran, Mr Arbuthnot. Ms Loughran is from our forensic division. Would you care to have a look at the body now?"

"Very well," he replied.

Loughran nodded to one of the men who was in charge of the corpse, and he drew back the blue cotton blanket that had been covering the face of the dead man. Arbuthnot leaned in a little over the gurney to get a good look.

"Well?" Lyons said.

"I can't say I recognise him. Not at all," Arbuthnot said, stepping back a couple of paces.

"Are you certain, sir?" Lyons said.

"Yes, Inspector, I am certain. Now, when are you going to let me get this place open again? The show must go on, as they say."

Loughran picked up the thread of the conversation, remembering Lyons' call with her partner earlier.

"We could be here for the rest of the day," she said, and noticed Arbuthnot getting redder in the face, no doubt preparing for some outburst. She went on quickly, "But I don't think that's really necessary in this case. Once we've tidied our things away and the body has been removed, you can have it back."

"Excellent! I'll make the arrangements then," he said and hurried off full of self-importance, using his mobile phone to get things moving.

Séan Mulholland, who had been keeping his distance, walked over to where Lyons was standing.

"God, Maureen, you two led him a right merry dance. I know he's a bit up himself, but he's not the worst of them, I can tell you."

"Don't worry, Séan, he'll get over it. But listen, the dead man must either be a local, or he's here for the festival and staying at one of the hotels or guest houses in the town. Can you get someone to ring around and see if there's anyone missing who didn't come home last night as expected?"

"Yes, of course. I'll get Peadar and Jim to start on it. Are we finished here?" Mulholland said as the black Mercedes van disappeared around the corner with its tragic cargo.

"Yes. I have to get back for the post-mortem. I'll take a photograph of Marquee Man when Dr Dodd has made him look a little less dead and send it to you if you want to circulate it around the town," Lyons said.

"Grand, thanks. I'll give you a call if there are any developments."

Lyons said goodbye to Loughran, thanking her for coming out to the scene.

"Sorry we couldn't find a bit more for you to go on, Maureen. Fancy a drink later on after work?" Loughran said.

"Maybe. Let's see how the PM goes and I'll give you a shout."

With that, they got into their respective vehicles and set off for the city.

* * *

Garda Pascal Brosnan ran the small Garda station in Roundstone with his colleague Garda Mary Fallon. The station had moved in 2003 from an old building at the end of the main street to a new, purpose-built premises adjacent to the Catholic church at the edge of the town.

Mary Fallon had originally been allocated to Clifden Garda station when she graduated from the training college in Templemore, but Séan Mulholland wasn't used to working with female officers, so he diverted her to Roundstone where she joined Pascal Brosnan who had up to that time run the facility single-handedly. She was a pretty woman, and there had been some rumours in circulation about a romantic relationship between herself and Brosnan, but it had never been substantiated. But they did get along very well, and were a very effective team.

The two Gardaí were just sitting down to a mid-morning cup of tea when the phone rang.

"It's always the bloody same," Brosnan said, getting up from the table and going to his desk to answer the call.

"Roundstone Gardaí," he said into the receiver.

"Oh, hello, Pascal, is it?" the woman's voice said.

"Yes, it is. Who is calling please?" he said, rolling his eyes at his colleague who giggled a little.

"Hello, Pascal. It's Agnes Feeney here from the Seaview guest house at Ervallagh. We're fierce busy with the festival in Clifden, Pascal. We have the place full to the rafters. But listen, there's something a bit funny. One of our guests didn't come back last night. Now he's all paid up, so that's not the problem. But his stuff is still in his room, and he's due to check out today. And I have the room booked again for tonight. What am I going to do, Pascal?" Mrs Feeney said.

"Maybe he just had a few too many pints last night out in Clifden, and he bedded down there for the night. He'll probably show up in an hour or two with a hangover to collect his belongings. Did he have a car?" Brosnan said.

"Oh, he did of course. You wouldn't get far out here without your own transport."

"Well, there you are then. He probably didn't want to drive after he'd had a few. I wouldn't worry too much about it. If he hasn't shown up by mid-afternoon, give us a call back here and we'll look into it. But just as you're here, what's the man's name?"

"He's a Mr Dunne, Adam Dunne."

"And do you have his car registration number by any chance?"

"Ah, now, Pascal, we haven't time to be looking for all that stuff when people arrive. It's only meself here, you know, in the afternoons. Paddy is out and about at that time."

"Righto, Mrs Feeney. Give me a call back later if he hasn't turned up. Thanks for your call."

"Oh, right, Pascal. I suppose I'll just gather his belongings up and keep them for him. But I don't like interfering with people's private stuff," Agnes Feeney said.

"It'll be fine, Mrs Feeney, don't worry."

Pascal Brosnan finished the call, and returned to the table where his tea was getting cold.

"What's wrong with her?" Mary Fallon asked.

Brosnan described the substance of the call to his colleague.

"Do we need to do anything?" Mary Fallon said.

"Ah, not at all. If he hasn't turned up by this evening, we can spring into action!" Brosnan said, sniggering a little.

Chapter Five

Maureen Lyons didn't enjoy post-mortems. Indeed, she knew no one that did, except for the pathologist himself, who seemed to have become immune to the process. It was the smell that got to her. This cadaver was fresh, but often that was not the case, and the heady mixture of formaldehyde, disinfectant and rotting flesh usually caused bile to rise to her mouth, so that she would have to excuse herself and get some clean fresh air outside in the car park.

But today, she was able to look on as Dodd paced around the shiny steel table that was supporting the man that had been brought in from the Clifden Arts Festival. He looked peaceful, lying there with his chest exposed and his eyes closed, with a muslin cloth covering his middle to grant what little dignity remained for the poor soul in death. Apart from the unnatural tone to his skin, Lyons thought that he could have just been asleep if she didn't know differently.

Dodd, now with a green rubber apron tied around his generous girth, and a blue cloth hat plastered down over his generous amount of dark hair, was making observations as he inspected the corpse, paying particular attention to the man's head. Lyons stood by, silent and expectant. He turned the man's head gently from left to right, and then took out a hand-held magnifying glass with a small ring of LED lights around the circumference and leant in close to the cadaver's face. He lifted the man's eyelids one at a time before standing back upright again.

"Hmm. I think we could be looking at asphyxia here, Inspector," he said to Lyons. "I'll know more when we've done the bloods and lungs, but there are what I would describe as promising signs. And there's something else. It looks like chummy here may have had some sort of mask pressed against his face too. There's an odd-looking indentation in the skin all around his mouth and nose. But let me get on, and I'll be able to tell you more in about an hour or so."

"Very well, Doctor. I'll go and have a word with Sinéad and see what she's up to. I'd like to have your complete opinion before I leave just in case it really is a suspicious death," Lyons said.

"Very well. Till later then," Dodd said, returning to his more gruesome task of opening up the man with a scalpel.

Lyons found Loughran at her bench in the laboratory behind the mortuary where she spent her day examining bits of evidence often recovered from crime scenes.

"Hi, Sinéad. What's the story?" Lyons said.

Loughran looked up from her work.

"Oh, hi, Maureen. Are you here for the PM?"

"Yes, and anything else I can establish. The doc says he thinks it might have been asphyxia. Just my luck," Lyons said.

"Well, he's not usually wrong, I'm afraid. Oh, by the way, I've sent Marquee Man's prints off to Dublin to see if they have any sign of him on any of their systems. There was no ID whatsoever on him, and I'm dying to know who he is, or was!"

"Me too. But what I was really hoping for was a nice cup of your famous filter coffee, Sinéad. Any chance?"

"Of course. Give me a minute."

Loughran busied herself rinsing out the jug from the coffee machine and filling the filter paper with two generous dessert spoons of Lavazza Rossa ground coffee, before putting water into the contraption and switching it on. After a moment or two it started to make satisfying gurgling noises.

"By the way, I was showing that little plastic collar thing we brought in from the site to my assistant Keith. He reckons it's from some sort of domestic product, like WD-40 or something."

"Oh, right. I suppose that might give us something to go on. Any maker's name or code number on it?"

"Keith says there's a number stamped into the thing, but it's tiny, and doesn't mean anything to him anyway."

"Typical. Nice coffee by the way," Lyons said, sipping the hot beverage.

As they were finishing their drinks, Dr Julian Dodd entered the room.

"Well, ladies, I was right. Your client out there was indeed asphyxiated, but it's a very unusual case. It seems that nitrogen was the weapon of choice in this instance. Very odd," the doctor said.

"Nitrogen! Cripes, I haven't come across that before. Are you sure, Doctor?" Lyons said.

"Inferior vena cava 88%; left ventricle 86%; right lung 85%; left lung 87%; alveolar air 96%, Inspector. The science doesn't lie," he said, a little indignantly.

"How the hell was that administered?" Lyons said.

"That, dear lady, is for you to determine. I'm just a humble pathologist." With that, he turned and left the room.

"Don't mind him, Maureen. He's all excited about a lot of new equipment he's been given recently. We don't have to send samples away to Dublin anymore for analysis. And he wouldn't say it was nitrogen if he wasn't sure."

"I don't disbelieve him, Sinéad. It's just he can be a bit insufferable at times. Surely you find that too?" Lyons said.

"I'm saying nothing. But why do you think I need a drink some evenings after I've finished up here?"

They both laughed.

"Look, I'd better get going. Can you do some research on this for us? Try and find out how someone would administer nitrogen out in the middle of nowhere. Then we'll see if we can establish some kind of motive."

"OK, will do. I'll catch you later."

"Great. Thanks."

Chapter Six

Pascal Brosnan and Mary Fallon were getting ready to lock up the Garda station in Roundstone when the phone rang. Fallon answered it with the usual salutation.

"Oh, hello, Guard. It's Agnes Feeney here again from Ervallagh. I'm just calling because Mr Dunne still hasn't shown up, and I'm fierce worried about him. I've taken all his stuff out of his room like Garda Brosnan said, but he should have come to collect them by now, and the new people are already checked into his room."

"I see. Well thanks for calling, Mrs Feeney. I'll let the Sergeant in Clifden know about it, and if he needs to talk to you, he'll give you a ring. It's Sergeant Mulholland," Fallon said.

"And is there nothing more at all I can do, Guard?"

"No, I don't think so. Did Pascal... eh Garda Brosnan, get an address from you for Mr Dunne?"

"Let me see. He did write it in our visitors book when he arrived, but I can't read the writing at all, except that I think the last bit is Dublin. And there's no phone number or anything, or car registration."

"OK, well don't worry, Mrs Feeney. You can leave it to us now, and thanks for the update."

When Mary Fallon had finished the call, she said to her colleague, "God, Pascal, she's very worried about this Dunne fella. And it is a bit odd, I suppose, that he hasn't turned up. Maybe I should drop into Clifden when I get back and tell Sergeant Mulholland. What do you think?"

"Yeah, you're probably right. There might be something in it, I suppose. Do you mind?"

"No, it's no bother. I'll get going then. Are you OK to finish up here?"

"Yes, sure. You get off."

Mary Fallon lived in a rented apartment close to the Garda station in Clifden. When she was transferred to Roundstone, she had already made a long-term arrangement with the landlady in Clifden, and she didn't like to break it so quickly. In any case, she enjoyed the thirty-minute journey in from Clifden every morning. She normally chose to drive along by the coast, through Ballyconneely where the Atlantic was either a beautiful aquamarine blue, or a steely grey, crashing against the rocks.

When she got to Clifden, she parked her VW Polo outside her place, and walked across to the Garda station. She went directly into the back office, where Sergeant Séan Mulholland was tidying up, getting ready to walk up the town to Cusheen's Bar, where he normally partook of two or three pints of Guinness while he perused the newspapers before driving home to his rather shabby bungalow out on the Sky Road.

"Hello, Sergeant," Fallon said as she entered the room.

"Ah, 'tis yourself, Mary. How's everything going out at Roundstone? I hope Pascal is behaving himself."

"Everything's grand thanks, Sergeant. I just popped in to tell you that we've had a Mrs Feeney ringing us today. She runs a bed and breakfast place out at Ervallagh, and one of her guests didn't come back last night. She seemed to be quite upset by it, but I doubt if it's that unusual."

"Maybe not, but I suppose you know there was a man found dead out at the showgrounds this morning. Very mysterious. Just lying there like he was asleep, he was. Inspector Lyons has been out and all. They've taken him away to Galway," Mulholland said.

"Crikey! I wonder if it's the same bloke. Do you have his name or anything?" Fallon said.

"Hang on a minute. No, we haven't any identification for him yet, but Inspector Lyons is sending out a photograph shortly and that will help us to find out who he was. Did your Mrs Feeney give you a name for her missing guest?"

"Yes, she did. It's Adam Dunne."

"Do you have any more details, like an address for this Dunne chap?" Mulholland said.

"No. She said she couldn't read the address he wrote in her visitors book, except that it was Dublin somewhere."

"Maybe I'll give Inspector Lyons a ring and get her to speed up the photograph. That might help."

"Would you mind? Then I suppose I'll have to traipse back into Ervallagh and visit Mrs Feeney to get confirmation, or not, that it's the same person," Mary Fallon said.

"Would Pascal not go around to her? We can send on the photo to him when it arrives."

"Ah, no, I'd better go myself. He asked me to look after the matter, and I wouldn't like to disturb his evening. It could all be a misunderstanding after all."

"OK. Well, let me give Maureen a call and see what she's got."

Mulholland made the call to Lyons, updating her with the information he had received from Mary Fallon, and requesting a photograph of the man.

Mulholland told her that the pictures would be with them straight away, and as if to confirm it, the office PC pinged to announce the arrival of an incoming message.

"Here, Mary, can you get these printed off? I'm not much good with this new-fangled technology. I usually get one of the lads to do it for me."

"Sure. Is the printer turned on?"

"Have a look yourself there. It probably is."

Mary Fallon checked the printer and clicked the mouse on the office PC a few times and in a few seconds the photographs started to emerge on A4 sheets. She waited for them to dry off before collecting them.

"You'd better give me a few of those too, Mary, and I'll see if anyone from the town recognises him, or can tell us his business here at the festival."

Fallon handed over a few of the printouts and said, "Right, I'll be off then. I'll let you know what Mrs Feeney says."

"Thanks, Mary. You can call me on my mobile phone if I've locked up by the time you get to see her. Though, maybe with this thing going on, I'd better keep the place open a bit later than usual tonight."

* * *

It took Mary Fallon just over forty minutes to get to Ervallagh. The sun was setting in the west, and a deep orange glow filled the sky, reflected on the peaceful waters of the Atlantic Ocean, as Fallon pulled her VW Polo up outside the unimaginatively named 'Sea View' guest house run by Mrs Agnes Feeney and her husband. There were three cars parked on the expansive tarmac in front of the property which had the traditional three arches to the front – a design that pervaded the area in the 1980s. The house had been extended, with guest rooms stretching away from the original bungalow both to the left and right, and Fallon calculated that Mrs Feeney could probably accommodate up to twenty residents in busy periods.

The front door to the house was propped open, but an inner glazed door was firmly shut with a notice in handwriting on a small square of white paper taped to the glass instructing visitors to 'push the bell once and wait'. Mary Fallon did as instructed.

After a few moments a rotund woman with a cheery red face and short, grey hair, who was dressed in a floral pinafore, approached from the locked side of the door and opened it.

"Hello, Mrs Feeney," Fallon said, guessing correctly at the woman's identity. "My name is Mary Fallon from Roundstone Garda. May I come in for a moment please?"

Mrs Feeney looked back down along the hall of her guest house, as if to check that there was no one observing, and then invited Fallon in. She ushered the Garda into a large room to the left of the hallway that had dual aspect windows, and looked out over the little strand to sea, validating the name of the establishment.

There were several easy chairs dotted around the room, a large flat-screen television which was mercifully switched off, and no other occupants. Feeling the need to explain the emptiness of the room to Fallon, Mrs Feeney said, "They'll all be upstairs having a rest or freshening up for another wee while, before they come down to watch the telly. We have all the channels here, you know." Mrs Feeney beamed with pride and gestured for Fallon to sit down. She selected one of the easy chairs upholstered in maroon velvet.

"Mrs Feeney, I understand you're concerned about a guest who didn't come back last night. A Mr Dunne, was it?" Fallon said.

"Yes, that's right. It sometimes happens that guests stay out when they have booked and paid for a room here, but they always show up the following day, even if it's only to collect their belongings. But Mr Dunne never appeared. I don't know what to do with his stuff."

Mary Fallon took out the folded A4-sized photograph from her inside jacket pocket and opened it up, offering it to Agnes Feeney.

"Would this be Mr Dunne, do you think, Mrs Feeney?"

Agnes Feeney reached into her apron pocket and took out a pair of spectacles and put them on. She studied the photograph carefully before handing it back.

"Well, it's not a very good likeness, and why are his eyes closed? But, yes, that's the man all right. Do you know where he is?" she said rather cautiously.

"I'm afraid this gentleman was found out at the showgrounds in Clifden earlier today, Mrs Feeney, and I'm sorry to say he is deceased."

Agnes Feeney looked intently at Mary Fallon for a moment, and her eyes widened.

"Good God! Are you serious?"

"Yes, I'm afraid so. We think he passed away sometime last night, but he wasn't found till this morning."

"Dear heavens, that's terrible. What took him, do you know? Was it a heart attack or something? He looked healthy enough to me."

"We're not sure just yet, Mrs Feeney. We're still looking into it. Would you mind if I had a look at the register where he signed in?" Fallon said.

"No, of course not. It's out at reception. Come on and I'll show you."

The two women got up and went to a small desk that was discreetly located in an alcove in the hallway with a telephone, a lamp, and the hard-backed visitors book perched on top.

Mary Fallon studied the entry that Dunne had made, but couldn't decipher the details, so she took out her phone and took a close-up photograph of the page.

"I think it might be best if I took Mr Dunne's luggage away with me, Mrs Feeney. There may be something in there that will give us an address or something. Do you have it handy?"

"What? Oh, sorry, yes, it's here behind the desk. I just bundled it all up and put it in his suitcase. I had to get the room ready for new guests today, you see."

"That's fine. Did you have much of a chat with Dunne when he arrived?" Fallon asked.

"No. It was busy at the time with other people checking in, so I just asked him to register and gave him his key, and pointed him in the direction of his room. But he seemed nice enough."

"Did you by any chance see what kind of car he was driving?"

"I'm sorry, but I didn't notice. God, this is terrible. It's never happened before, you know."

"I know, it's not pleasant for any of us. But if it's OK with you, I'll just take this and be away. There's a lot to do," Fallon said.

Chapter Seven

Maureen Lyons had got back to the Garda HQ in Galway's Mill Street late in the afternoon. As soon as she arrived, Detective Sergeant Sally Fahy followed her into her office.

"Hi, boss. Do you need a coffee or something? You've been gone all day," Fahy said, thoughtful as ever.

Sally Fahy was a young DS who had at one time been a civilian worker in the Galway Garda offices. She enjoyed the work so much that she had applied to join, and after her training in Templemore, Superintendent Mick Hays had pulled a few strings and got her assigned to the team back in Galway. She had quickly proved her worth, and had been promoted following a very successful, but highly dangerous arrest of a jewel thief in a shop in the city centre who was armed and ready to kill. The only regret Fahy had about joining the Gardaí was that she hadn't, as yet, met the love of her life.

"No, I'm OK thanks, Sally. But could you round up Eamon for me and ask Sinéad to come across. I want to have a team meeting in fifteen minutes about things out west."

"Yes, sure. Do you want John O'Connor too?"

"Yes, why not."

Fahy left and went to make the arrangements.

Lyons lifted the phone and called upstairs to her partner, Mick Hays.

"Hi, Mick. It's me. How's things?"

"Ah, so-so. You know how it is. More paperwork than is good for me, but I'm getting through it at last. What have you been up to?"

"I've been out with Séan Mulholland for most of the day. That death out at the arts festival in Clifden looks suspicious, and I'm just getting started on it. I'm thinking maybe this guy had a dodgy past that has finally caught up with him. What time will you be finished this evening?" Lyons said.

"I'd say in about an hour, as long as Plunkett doesn't catch me on the way out. I think there's something going on with budgets, and he's like a hen on a hot griddle with it all."

"Nothing new there then. If you can escape in an hour, do you fancy getting something to eat out? I'm not in the mood for slaving over a hot stove tonight," Lyons said.

"Yeah, why not. Sounds good. Let me get on here and I'll give you a call when I'm almost done," Hays said.

"Great. See ya."

* * *

"OK, everyone, listen up," Lyons said when she came back into the main office. She stood at the top of the room beside the whiteboard that the detectives used to work out ideas about the case they were handling, and make connections. She had asked Sinéad Loughran to come across and join the briefing too.

"It's now virtually certain that Mr Adam Dunne was murdered last night out at the arts festival in Clifden. But so far, we have very little to go on, other than we think he was asphyxiated with nitrogen gas."

The team exchanged puzzled looks.

"Yes, I know, it's very unusual, but that's what Dr Dodd said, and he was pretty insistent. Sinéad, do we have anything more?" Lyons said.

"No, not yet in any case, Inspector. It's more what we didn't find than what we did that's bothering me."

"For instance?" Lyons said.

"He had no mobile phone, no car keys, no wallet, or any form of ID on him, which is pretty strange, don't you think?"

"Yes, I guess so. But Mary Fallon is collecting his suitcase from the guest house he was staying at near Roundstone. She's going to drop it off first thing tomorrow. When it gets here, Sinéad, can you give it a good going over and see what we can find out about him?"

"Yes, I'll give Mary a call later and fix it up," Loughran said.

Garda John O'Connor raised his hand.

"Yes, John," Lyons said.

"I could do a trawl on the internet for any sign of him. You know, Facebook, Instagram, Twitter – that sort of thing. And I could have a look at the driving licenses and the other government sites too. He might be on benefits or something," the young Garda said.

There was nothing O'Connor liked more than spending time with technology. He was usually very successful at tracing people and their movements and interests, and the more challenging it was, the better he liked it.

"OK. Good idea, John. And while you're at it, have a go at the mobile phone companies too. I know it's a long shot, but maybe one of them has an Adam Dunne whose phone was in the Clifden area over the last few days."

"OK, boss, but that could take a while. There must be hundreds of Adam Dunnes with mobiles. But I'll see what I can do."

"Thanks, John. Eamon, I'd like you to concentrate on his car. Mrs Feeney, the woman who runs the guest house where he was staying, says he had one. Sinéad, did you find any car keys on him or near him on the ground anywhere?"

"No, 'fraid not. But I was thinking. Maybe we need to go back out to the site early doors tomorrow before the festival gets going and do a better search of the area. Inspector Flynn could come out too and try and find his car," Loughran said, looking at Inspector Eamon Flynn.

"Good idea. Make sure to keep Séan Mulholland informed. And he may have some results from his enquiries locally too. You can liaise with a Mathew Arbuthnot at the festival. He runs the whole show out there it seems. But don't take any shit from him. He's not easy."

"Right, Sinéad," Eamon Flynn said, "why don't we muster here at eight o'clock tomorrow? Can we take your big jeep?"

"Sure, and if you buy me a white coffee with two sugars, I'll even let you play with the flashing lights and the siren!" Loughran said, cheekily.

"Deal!" Flynn replied, smiling.

"Why don't you arrange to go via Roundstone and collect Dunne's bag from Mary Fallon while you're at it? It will save her a journey, and you can go that way into Clifden," Lyons said.

"Yes, good idea, I'll give her a call and set that up," Loughran replied.

When Lyons got back to her own office, she called Mick Hays.

"Hi. Are you nearly ready for off?" she said.

"Good timing. I'm just finished. What do you fancy?" Hays said.

"I was wondering if we could try that new place down on Cross Street? I think it's called Deep Blue. It's a seafood restaurant, and I've heard good reports about it."

"Sounds like a plan. I'll see you downstairs in a couple of minutes."

"Great."

Chapter Eight

Mick Hays and Maureen Lyons left the Mill Street Garda station together at half past six. It was a mild evening, but there were thick grey clouds lingering over the city, and it wouldn't be long before heavy showers, so typical of early autumn in Galway, fell from the sky. There was a slight chill in the air too, as often preceded the rain at that time of year.

But there were still a good few people out and about, some carrying large paper carrier bags full of clothes bearing the names of popular outlets in the city. Others on their way home from work hurried along, keen to reach their cars and get indoors before the deluge.

The Deep Blue restaurant was positioned over a large pharmacy on the narrow street that connects Middle Street to the roundabout at the junction of Bridge Street and Lombard Street. Cross Street was festooned with eateries of every kind, from Chinese takeaways to posh restaurants, all packed in tightly between other commercial properties and even a few private apartments. They found Deep Blue easily enough, and entered via a stairway into a small vestibule where decals on the glass partitions boasted 'Galway's newest and finest fresh seafood'.

The two of them stood there for a minute, until a young waiter in a black apron approached carrying two large, laminated menus.

"Table for two?" he enquired.

"Yes, please. By the window if you have it," Hays said.

They took their seats at a rather small table overlooking the street.

"So, how's things going with your Marquee Man case out west?" Hays asked when they were settled.

"Not terribly well, if truth be told. All we know is that the deceased doesn't appear to be a local man. But we've no idea who bumped him off or why. Not yet in any case. And another thing, Dodd says he was asphyxiated with nitrogen. I haven't come across that before, have you?"

"Crikey! Yes, I have as it happens. I was reading a little while back that somewhere in the United States, Alabama, I think, they are talking of using nitrogen to carry out executions. It's called nitrogen hypoxia. Basically it deprives the subject of oxygen, and they pass out almost instantly and don't recover."

"And what's the big advantage?" Lyons said.

"It's cheap, apparently, and very effective."

Just then, the waiter reappeared with a nicely chilled bottle of wine, and made quite a performance of opening it and offering a tincture for Hays to test. Hays nodded, and the lad poured a decent measure into Maureen's glass before topping up Hays'. He left the remainder of the bottle in a floor-standing wine cooler, and covered it with a white linen cloth.

"Cheers, anyway," Lyons said, holding up her glass which Hays touched with his own.

"There might be a Dublin connection to this thing too, though I'm not sure what just yet. Do you know anyone well up there that we could get to do a little snooping for us?" Lyons said.

"No problem. But I'd prefer to have a bit more information first. Can you wait till the investigation has moved on a bit, and then I'll call in a few favours?"

"Yes, OK."

The waiter returned with two plates of delicious food, and wished them *bon appétit.*

Hays and Lyons enjoyed the meal. "We must come here again. What do you think?" Lyons said.

"I agree. Fantastic grub. Do you fancy a dessert?" Hays said.

"I do, but I won't. A girl has to look after her figure, you know."

"Hmm... coffee back at home then," he said, a little disappointed. He had spotted one of his favourite desserts on the menu, and was hoping to try it out, but it was not to be.

* * *

The rain had moved on by the next morning when Sinéad Loughran and Eamon Flynn met at the Garda station. It was a cool, clear, autumn day with just a light breeze to remind you that winter was approaching.

"Hi, Sinéad," Flynn said climbing into the passenger's seat in the front of Loughran's Toyota Landcruiser.

Loughran was looking well, as always, with her shoulder-length blonde hair tied back in a ponytail, and her makeup sparingly applied to her pretty face.

"Hi, Eamon. Where's my coffee?"

"Oh, shit, I totally forgot. Sorry."

"Never mind. But that's the first stop on the way out to Clifden. And you can get me a bun as well for being so forgetful," she teased, with a broad smile on her face.

"Fair enough. The gas station at the start of the N59 serves coffee, I think, and they're bound to have some snacks."

"Right, well let's get going then," she said as he closed the door, and she gunned the big jeep away from the station entrance.

"Cripes, you don't hang around, do you, Sinéad?"

"Don't tell anyone, but this vehicle is the main reason I joined forensics. I love it. And you should see me when I really get going!"

"Eh... it's OK thanks, and I don't believe a word of it."

"Well, maybe not the only reason, but I do love driving it. I got back into town from Clifden in forty-eight minutes yesterday, and I hardly touched the brakes."

"Well, we're in no hurry this morning, so spare a thought for your passenger!"

They stopped at the big Circle K petrol station at the start if the N59 heading west from Galway, and as promised Flynn procured two hot coffees, but the place couldn't offer any food at that time of day. It was too early. When they had finished their drink, they set off again, but Loughran kept the vehicle at a modest speed, not wishing to put the wind up her colleague.

"Shall we go in via Roundstone, Eamon, and collect Dunne's suitcase, or would you prefer to do that on the way back?" Loughran said as they drove through Moycullen, which wasn't really awake at that hour of the morning.

"Let's collect it on the way out. Then, if we have any spare time in Clifden we can go through it out there," Flynn said.

"Good idea."

As they left Oughterard behind, crossed the Owenriff River and continued up the hill onto the heathland, the sun was starting to shine in the cloudless sky. The numerous lakes along the roadside looked like shimmering silver in the sunlight, and the heather, now in full bloom, coloured the bog in a magnificent deep mauve colour, beautifully offset by the blue of the mountains in the distance. Loughran pressed on a little more quickly on the deserted road, and the big 4x4 soaked up the undulations in comfort. As they passed the Anglers Return, close to Ballynahinch Castle, where the road was more sheltered, fuchsia bushes were coming into bloom with their bright red and purple trumpet-shaped flowers. They crossed Roundstone Bog, past Tadgh Deasy's motor works, and soon arrived in Roundstone, which was still very quiet in the early morning sunshine.

Loughran pulled the Toyota up outside the Garda station at the edge of the village, pleased to see that Mary Fallon's little silver VW Polo was parked outside.

Chapter Nine

Inside the small station Pascal Brosnan and Mary Fallon were just going through the day's plans.

"Hi, Mary; Pascal. I don't suppose we could scam a cup of tea? I'm parched after the drive out, and I didn't get a chance for a proper breakfast this morning," Sinéad Loughran said.

"Of course. No bother," Pascal replied, "and I think we might be able to rustle up a Danish pastry for you. It's still fresh. I only got them yesterday afternoon."

"You're a saint, Pascal," Loughran said.

When Pascal had gone to the tiny kitchenette at the back of the building to prepare the refreshments, Eamon Flynn spoke to Mary Fallon.

"I believe you have yer man's suitcase from the guest house at Ervallagh, Mary. Anything interesting in it?"

"Gosh, I didn't like to go through it, Inspector. I thought Sinéad would like to get at it first, for forensics. Did I do wrong?" Fallon said, her pretty face flushing visibly.

"No, not at all. Quite right. Could you get it for us, and we'll let Sinéad loose on it?"

Mary Fallon opened a large cupboard that ran underneath the counter of the Garda station, and retrieved a modestly sized wheeled suitcase in a rather unpleasant shade of green. It had a pull-out handle at the top, and illegible remnants of some travel stickers dotted here and there on the outer surface.

Loughran donned the familiar nitrile gloves and lifted the case up onto the table. She unzipped it gingerly, and lifted the lid up a few centimetres, bending down to peep inside, before opening it fully to reveal the contents.

The case contained a number of items of clothing; a washbag with razor, toothpaste and a toothbrush; and a small plastic bag with used underwear and socks which Loughran chose not to explore. She lifted the clothing out of the case and started to examine the lining, paying particular attention to the place where it was fixed to the frame close to the opening lid. Mary Fallon looked on, fascinated, as Sinéad Loughran picked at a place on the lining and was able to pull it away from the body of the case sufficiently to get her hand inside. She felt around for a second or two, and then withdrew three maroon-coloured booklets which were obviously passports.

"Wow! I'd never have found those, Sinéad. Nice one!" Fallon said.

Pascal Brosnan came back into the room carrying a tray with four mugs of steaming tea and a plate with several Danish pastries piled up on it.

"There you go – breakfast," he said.

"Thanks, Pascal. Just what the doctor ordered."

"So, can we see who owns the passports, Sinéad?" Flynn said as he finished his snack, and licked his fingers to remove the sticky residue left by the cake.

Loughran spread the three passports out on the table and opened the first one.

"Well, this is an Irish passport in the name of Adam Dunne, and if I'm not mistaken, the photo is of the bloke we found in the marquee. It was issued three years ago in Dublin."

"And the next one?" Flynn asked.

Loughran picked up the second passport and studied the cover briefly.

"This is a British passport." Opening the little booklet, she went on, "And it was issued to an Alan Dickson five years ago. Same bloke in the photo, just looking a bit younger."

"And the third?" Flynn said.

"This one is belonging to Anselm Dargan. It's the oldest one, in fact it expires soon, and yer man is looking a lot younger and very shifty in it." She held up the photo page of the passport for them all to see.

"Hmm... I see what you mean. Any stamps in any of them? You know, the brand that the passport control people put in them."

Loughran went back through the three passports, flicking the pages to see if there were any entry or exit stamps in any of them.

"Yes, here we are. The Alan Dickson one has stamps for Zimbabwe. Let's see, entered Harare last year, and it looks as if he was there for just a few days. Then he was back again this year, again for a few days."

Loughran put down the Alan Dickson passport and picked up one of the others.

"And Adam Dunne has been to Australia too. Earlier this year again. He went in through Melbourne and came out of Sydney."

"How long was he there for?" Flynn asked.

"Again, just a few days. From the fourteenth of May to the nineteenth," Loughran said.

"Seems like a long way to go for five days. I wonder what he was up to," Flynn said.

"I'll bag these up if that's OK, Eamon, and take them back to the lab. I'd like to see if these are the real deal or forgeries. I don't know anyone with several passports. And promise me, if there's a trip to Africa in connection with this case, I'm coming with you," Loughran said with a twinkle in her eyes.

"Fat chance. More like South Galway, and you're welcome to that, any day!"

Flynn and Loughran finished their tea and cakes, and took the suitcase and its contents away with them; thanking Fallon and Brosnan for their hospitality, they set off for Clifden.

As they drove along the old bog road towards Murvey and Ballyconneely, the sun, now higher in the autumn sky, glinted off the rocks along the roadside. When they got as far as Ballyconneely, the deep aquamarine blue of the Atlantic Ocean gently lapping on the golden sandy shore made a magnificent sight in the mid-morning sunshine.

* * *

At Clifden Garda station, Sergeant Séan Mulholland was himself having a mug of strong tea, accompanied by his signature Goldgrain biscuits that were his any-time-of-day snack.

"Ah, good morning, folks. Can I get you a cuppa this fine morning?" he said cheerily as Flynn and Loughran came in.

"No, thanks, Séan," Flynn said, "we've just been in Roundstone and we were fed and watered there."

"Oh, right, so. Listen, wait till I tell you," Mulholland said, taking up his tea and moving into the rear of the premises which was a lot more private. "One of our lads was out around the town earlier. You know, just doing a walkabout to make sure everything was in order. You can't be too careful with the festival on."

"OK. And...?" Flynn said, finding it a little difficult adjusting to the pace of the older man who never seemed to be in a hurry.

"Well, as he was walking past the butcher's shop, Finn Gilpin, he's the man that runs the place, called him in. He pointed out a silver VW Passat that was parked almost directly outside his shop. He said it had been there for three days, and the funny thing is, the key was still in the ignition."

"What did Gilpin do?" Flynn asked.

"He showed Finn the photo of Marquee Man, and Finn was fairly sure it was him who parked the car there a few days back."

"I see," Flynn said. "So, the car probably belongs to the deceased. That's handy. Did your man get the registration number?"

"Oh, he did of course," Mulholland said. He went to his desk and was visibly pleased when he was quickly able to locate a scrap of paper with the number on. He handed it to Flynn.

"Have you looked this up on the system, Séan?" Flynn said.

"Eh... no, not yet. But you can use this computer here if you want to," Mulholland said, gesturing to a rather ancient-looking beige device with a large CRT monitor off to one side of the office.

Flynn walked over to where the computer sat with a weird set of coloured lines travelling randomly across the screen. He touched the mouse, and the PC sprang to life. Flynn sat down and called up the Garda vehicle information system. He tapped in the number that Mulholland had given him.

"Here we go. Adam Dunne, if you don't mind, and I have an address for him here as well. Do you know, Séan, if the car has a current tax and insurance disc?" Flynn said, looking over his shoulder.

"Eh... no, I'm not sure, but we can go and have a look at it if you like. It's only up the road."

"Tell you what, Séan. Do you know anyone hereabouts that could lift that car and bring it back to Galway for our forensic people to examine? I'm sure Sinéad here could set something up later today."

"Yes, that's no problem," Loughran interjected.

"I do. We could get Tadgh Deasy to do it. He has a truck with a crane, and we've used him before. Do you want me to give him a call?" Mulholland said.

"Yes, please. And while we're waiting for him to come out, I'd like you to post one of your lads down at the car to keep an eye on it in case someone decides to make off with it. Tell him not to let anyone touch it though. Except for Deasy of course."

"OK, Inspector, I'll get that organised right away."

"And, Séan, you can call me Eamon when it's just the three of us. 'Inspector' sounds too formal," Flynn said.

"Oh, right, so, Eamon," Mulholland said, and got busy making the arrangements.

Chapter Ten

Sinéad Loughran had gone off to find the butcher's shop and the abandoned VW, leaving Eamon Flynn in the Garda station. She wanted to see if there was anything visible about the car from the outside that she could start investigating, before it went back to the city to be pulled apart.

Flynn made a phone call to Maureen Lyons.

"Hi, Maureen. It's Eamon. I'm out here in Clifden and there have been some developments."

Flynn went on to tell Lyons about the passports that they had found in Adam Dunne's suitcase, and the car that was registered to the dead man and would soon be on its way back to Galway for a thorough technical examination.

"OK, Eamon. Give me the address you found when you looked up the car on the system and I'll get onto Dublin and get someone around to his house to see if we can find a relative or maybe even a wife. When will we have the car back?" Lyons said.

"Séan is getting someone called Deasy to haul it in for us. It shouldn't be too difficult. The key is still in it! Do we have Deasy's prints on file? He's bound to put his greasy paws all over it to get it up on his truck," Flynn said.

"Oh, we do indeed. We're well acquainted with Mr Deasy. But he can be useful sometimes."

"Great. Sinéad has just gone for a wander up the town to eyeball the vehicle. When she gets back, we'll head out to Galway, unless she wants to spend more time down at the scene, but I don't think she will. This business with the car has her all fired up."

"OK. See you in a while. Thanks," Lyons said.

When Eamon Flynn had finished the call, he spoke to Séan Mulholland.

"Séan, did any of your people find out anything else about the dead man in their enquiries around the town?"

"Ah, nothing much. The barman from the hotel up the road says he might have been in early on the night he died. But he couldn't be sure. It was fierce busy with visitors," Mulholland said.

"Did the barman say if there was anyone with him?"

"No, he didn't. As I said, the place was heaving, so he was busy pouring drinks."

"I don't suppose there's any CCTV in the hotel? If Marquee Man was with someone or meeting someone, it could give us a clue as to who killed him," Flynn said.

"Ah, away with ye, CCTV! Not at all, man. This isn't New York!"

"Yes, OK, sorry, Séan. But so far this case is a right old puzzle."

"Don't worry, Eamon. With Maureen Lyons and yourself on the case, it won't be long before you have a breakthrough."

* * *

Lyons took the details that Flynn had given her for the car that had been found abandoned outside the butcher's shop in Clifden. She called a colleague in Dublin's Pearse Street Garda station, and asked if they had anyone free to go and check an address.

"What's the address, Inspector?" the Garda from Dublin asked.

"It's 126, Elgin Road, Ballsbridge," she said.

"Oh, very nice. That's a very upmarket area. Righto, we'll get a car out there as soon as there's anyone free. Who are we looking for again?"

"Well, the owner of the car is Adam Dunne, but don't expect to find him there. We have him here at the mortuary. But he may have relatives at that address, so tell whoever is going out to take it easy."

"Understood. Can I call you back later?"

"Yes, please," Lyons said. She gave the man her contact details and finished the call.

With nothing to do until Flynn and Loughran got back to the city, Lyons spent an hour going through her emails and the several memos that she received every day from Garda HQ in the Phoenix Park in Dublin.

* * *

Lyons was just settling down to a cup of tea in her office when the phone rang.

"Lyons," she said.

"Hello, Inspector. This is Garda Sweetnam from Pearse Street. You were asking about an Adam Dunne who gave his address as 126, Elgin Road. Is that right?"

"Yes, that's right. Did you find anyone at home?" Lyons said.

"Eh, no, in fact we didn't find the house either. The numbers on Elgin Road stop at 72. There's no 126, and we had a good cruise around in case there might be a block of flats or something that would extend the numbers, but there isn't."

"I see. Any other ideas, Guard? That's definitely the address his car is registered to."

"It happens all the time, Inspector. Fellas think they can avoid parking tickets and speeding fines by putting a false address on the registration document, but it doesn't work. We get them in the end. Sorry we couldn't help."

"Not to worry, Guard. Thanks for trying anyway. Bye."

Lyons hung up. She was very puzzled. None of this made any sense. She did what she often found helpful in the past. She took a large sheet of A3 paper from the printer in the open plan, brought it back into her office and started to draw. She used a spider diagram with 'A.D.' in a circle in the centre, and lines leading out to other smaller circles containing 'Arts Festival'; 'Ervallagh'; 'VW car'; 'Nitrogen poisoning', and 'Elgin Road', and spent a few minutes studying her work. Unfortunately, nothing made any sense.

* * *

It was late afternoon, and she was just beginning to feel really fed up when Sinéad Loughran popped her head around the door.

"Hi, Maureen. Got a minute?" Loughran said.

"Hi, Sinéad, yes, of course, come in. How did you get on out beyond? I hope you have some good news for me. This thing is doing my head in."

"Well, prepare to be amazed," Loughran said, with a wide smile and a sparkle in her blue eyes.

Lyons looked at her colleague a little sceptically. She was quite familiar with Loughran's sense of humour.

"Go on," Lyons said.

"I know you like to bring me presents, Maureen, but this time you really have excelled yourself," she said, reaching into her handbag and taking out a small black velvet bag with a drawstring around the opening.

"What's that?" Lyons said, a little impatiently.

Loughran opened the mouth of the bag and gently tipped the contents out onto Lyons' A3 diagram. Two small, sparkling, clear stones tumbled out and rolled towards Lyons.

"Crikey! Where did you get those, Sinéad?"

"That's just it. They were hidden under the spare wheel in chummy's car. And that's not all. There was almost twenty-five thousand euro in used notes all nicely bundled up in blocks of five thousand as well. Obviously, I didn't bring that across with me. It's going straight to my bank account!"

"Blimey. Are these the real deal?" Lyons said.

"I think so. Now, I'm no expert, but they look like the genuine article to me. They'd make a nice ring, wouldn't they?"

"You're telling me. What are they worth?"

"If they are genuine diamonds, then plenty," Loughran said.

"So, our Mr Dunne, or whatever his name is, had quite a few big ones stashed in his open car on the main street of Clifden while he went off to get himself killed in an unusual fashion. Nice. Anything else from the car?"

"The lads are just going over it carefully now for prints, fibres and so on. But I think this is the mother lode, wouldn't you say?"

"I guess. What are you going to do with them now?" Lyons said.

"Well, if I had a decent bloke to my name, I'd obviously get them made into a fabulous engagement ring. But alas, 'tis not to be, so they go back in the evidence safe with the cash, and I s'pose you'll put an ad up in lost and found for anyone who has misplaced a couple of nice little diamonds."

"Perhaps not, Sinéad, but this thing just got a whole lot more interesting. But hang on. I think we need to get these in front of an expert who can tell us a bit more about them, don't you?"

"Probably a good idea. Know anyone?" Loughran said.

"I do, as it happens. The owner of Hardy's downtown is allegedly knowledgeable in this particular field. Why don't I ask him to pop over with his cute little jeweller's loupe for a look-see?"

"Great. I think I'd better wait with you, Maureen, in case one of these disappears into your purse," Loughran said, smiling again.

"OK. Hang on, I'll give Clive Richardson in Hardy's a call."

Loughran went off to make them both a cup of fresh tea while Lyons called the jewellers. Richardson, who had been most helpful to the Galway detectives in the past was only too pleased to be asked. In return for his expertise, he would get the occasional unofficial escort when he was carrying a consignment of valuable stock in his car.

Chapter Eleven

Lyons and Loughran had just finished their tea when Richardson arrived downstairs. Loughran went to fetch the man, and was back in a couple of minutes with him in tow.

The jeweller was a tall, slender man in his early fifties, immaculately dressed in a navy pinstripe suit, pale cream shirt and silk tie. Richardson's parents had escaped Nazi Germany at the start of the war and ended up in Ireland with few possessions, save for a small amount of gold jewellery that they had managed to smuggle out. They were originally called Kleinmann, but changed their surname to Richardson on arrival in Ireland to help disguise their origins, which was quite a usual practice then. Not that it mattered a great deal. Ireland was generally welcoming to fleeing Jews at that time, and many such refugees went on to set up good businesses all over the country.

When introductions had been made, Lyons invited Richardson to sit opposite her at her desk, alongside Sinéad Loughran.

"Thanks for coming over, Mr Richardson," Lyons said. "I wonder if you could have a look at these two stones that we have come across as part of an investigation."

She moved the two diamonds across the desk in front of the jeweller. As expected, he removed a small gold-coloured loupe from his jacket pocket, and took thin tweezers from his inside jacket pocket. Richardson gripped the first stone, put the glass to his eye and slowly turned the diamond around looking intently at it. Lyons and Loughran were almost holding their breath in anticipation.

Richardson placed the first stone back on the desk and repeated the procedure with the second one. Having examined the diamond carefully, he placed it gently back on the table and folded the loupe away.

"What you have here, ladies, are two of the very best quality diamonds I have ever come across. They are spectacular. Very clear, and the best possible colour."

"I see. How much do you think they are worth, Mr Richardson?" Loughran said.

"Well, I don't have my scales with me, but I'd estimate they are about 1.5 carats apiece. At this quality, if I'm right about the weight, they would be worth around fourteen or fifteen thousand euro each, wholesale. Retail, if they were worked into a ring, for example, they could be up to twenty thousand euro each."

"Wow! I'd no idea," Lyons said.

Richardson smiled.

"These are unusually good quality stones, Inspector. And that's quite rare. I know of several jewellers who would be very happy to have them in their safe."

"Where would they have come from, Mr Richardson?" Loughran said.

"Russia has the largest amount of diamond production these days, but these are of such high quality, I'd be more inclined to think Africa, maybe Zimbabwe or Angola, though I could be wrong, of course."

"And how does Zimbabwe sell diamonds?" Lyons asked.

"There are a number of outlets. They often hold diamond auctions in various cities such as Antwerp,

London, and New York. Of course, you have to be invited to attend, and only certified dealers are permitted in any case. Some big merchants buy direct from the mining companies too, but that's a bit unusual. DeBeers who used to control over eighty per cent of the world's diamond market are still very active as well. So, they could have come from anywhere really. But it's a bit unusual to find just two on their own like that. If they belong to a manufacturing jeweller, you'd expect there to be more of them. May I ask where you got them?" Richardson said.

"I'm sorry, Mr Richardson, I'm not at liberty to share that with you for now. Let's just say the circumstances in which they were discovered suggest criminality," Lyons said.

"I see. Does that mean you don't have any paperwork for them?"

"What paperwork would you expect?" Loughran said.

"All legitimate diamonds have to pass through a process known as the Kimberley Process. It was set up in 2003 by the UN to try to stop what are euphemistically known as 'conflict diamonds' circulating. All legitimately mined diamonds are certified as coming from a proper source. If they don't have that certification, then they could be blood diamonds," Richardson said.

"Blood diamonds?" Lyons said.

"Yes. Illegal currency used to fund war, or even terrorism. There's still quite a bit of it going on. No dealer or jeweller would touch these without their proper KP certificates."

Lyons looked at Loughran for an instant.

"Mr Richardson, would you have any ideas about any dodgy dealings going on around here involving stones?" Lyons said.

"Oh, no. Not like this anyway. As you know, if we get anyone in trying to offload stolen jewellery, we always call the Gardaí. I think we've helped you to nail a few of the local robbers. But these stones aren't the proceeds of a house break-in, in my view."

"Yes, I agree. Well, listen, if you do by any chance hear of anything unusual going on connected to loose diamonds, please give me a call," Lyons said. She handed him one of her business cards.

"Yes, of course, Inspector. Sorry not to be of more assistance," Richardson said, getting up to leave.

"Oh, no, you have been most helpful. Thanks again for coming across."

* * *

When Richardson had left, Lyons turned to her colleague. "What do you make of that, then?"

"God, I don't know, Maureen. It looks as if Marquee Man was mixed up in some very nefarious activity. But how did he manage to get himself bumped off? I'm glad it's your job to find that out, not mine."

"You're right. Why don't you get off back to your petri dishes, and leave me to sort this out. But let me know if you get anything more from the car. By the way, did we find Dunne's mobile phone or notebook PC, if he had one?"

"I don't know. I'll get back across the road and see what the lads have managed to dig up. I'll call you later on."

"Thanks, Sinéad. See ya."

When Loughran had left, Lyons went outside and found Sally Fahy and Eamon Flynn. She updated them with the information that she had been told by the jeweller.

"OK," Flynn said, "so Adam Dunne, or whoever he is, sorry, was, is somehow involved in the diamond trade, or at least, the shadier side of it. But how did that get him killed?"

"That's what we need to find out, Eamon. And, of course, who killed him. Let's start by doing a deep dive onto Dunne's background. Sally, can you start with the car? It's quite new. Get onto VW in Dublin, and see if they have a service record for it. If you can find out who serviced it last, get on to the garage and see if they have any information on the man, like his credit or debit card details, or mobile phone number. They might even have a genuine address for him."

"Yes, OK, boss," Fahy said.

"Eamon, I'd like you to concentrate on the diamonds. Find out if there's any history anywhere of diamond smuggling in Ireland. Contact the Park and ask them to see what they can find, if anything. And then get back onto Séan. I want to keep him on his toes. After all, the crime was committed on his patch. Make sure he's still on the case out there. Go back out if necessary."

"OK, Maureen. Do you think there's any connection between the Arts Festival and the murder?" Flynn said.

"That's what we need to find out. I'm going to focus on whatever Sinéad can come up with from his car, and the stuff in his suitcase. Let's meet back at close of play to compare notes. If you're still out west, Eamon, give us a call around five-thirty. OK, everyone, let's get going."

Chapter Twelve

Lyons was back in her office when her phone rang. It was Sinéad Loughran.

"Hi, Maureen. I thought I'd give you a call to tell you what was found in the car. There was a mobile phone tucked away out of sight behind the glove box. I'm just getting it charged up now so we can interrogate it. And there was a business card for a Vincent Henderson, and the name of a hotel in Clifden scribbled on the reverse side. It's the Alcock and Brown. But there's something else too."

"What's that, Sinéad?" Lyons said.

"We found traces of resin in the back of the car on the floor mat. It looks like shavings, or maybe where a drill was used on something," Loughran said.

"What kind or resin is it?"

"I'm not sure. Some form of synthetic stuff. I'll have it analysed and see what we can determine. By the way, can you drop the diamonds over? I need to put them back in the evidence safe."

"I don't have them, Sinéad, I gave them to you," Lyons said.

There was a deafening silence from the other end of the line.

"Eh, no, you didn't. I left them with you, Maureen."

"No. I gave them back to you when Richardson left. I put them in the little pouch and handed them to you. I remember clearly."

"Hang on a sec."

Loughran put the phone down on the desk, and Lyons could hear her rummaging. She was back on the line a few moments later.

"No, listen, hun, I really don't have them. I remember you giving me the pouch, but the stones were still out on the desk. I'm certain," Loughran said in a rather serious voice.

"Well, they're not here now. Are you sure you don't have them, Sinéad? Have another look in your handbag," Lyons said. She was beginning to get a very unpleasant feeling in the pit of her stomach. She waited patiently for her colleague to repeat the search in her bag.

"No, definitely not. You don't think Richardson might have taken them, do you?"

"Not a chance. I saw them on the desk after he was gone, but I'm sure I put them back in the little pouch and handed it to you."

"Fuck it, Maureen, we can't have lost them. This is stupid. What are we going to do?" Loughran said.

"Well, let's not panic. They have to be somewhere. I'll have a good look around here, and you do the same over there. Give me a call back if you find them," Lyons said.

"OK, bye."

Lyons searched carefully all around her desk, but found nothing. She looked in her desk drawers, in case the little stones might have fallen in, but they hadn't. Then she moved the chair back from her desk and got down on the floor. She used the light from her phone to illuminate the dark area beneath her desk, and searched all around. The diamonds were nowhere to be seen. She scrambled back to a seating position and stopped to think. Then she lifted the phone and called Mick Hays.

"Hi, Mick. Listen, can I pop up for a few minutes? It's a bit urgent."

"Yes, of course. Is everything OK?" Hays said.

"Not really, no. I'll tell you when I see you."

"OK. No problem."

Five minutes later Lyons was seated in front of Mick Hays at his spacious mahogany desk, which was more cluttered than usual. She told her partner about the missing diamonds and waited for his response, which came when he had deliberated for a few tense moments.

"OK, well the way I see it, there are two, or maybe three, problems here. Firstly, these diamonds are critical evidence in what is very likely a murder case. Secondly, there's the fact that these things are obviously very valuable, and that's a big problem. And thirdly, it's not clear who actually had charge of the stones when they went missing. And as it's between you and Sinéad, this is potentially going to cause a nasty rift in your friendship. Have I missed anything?" Hays said.

"Jesus, Mick, don't sugar coat it whatever you do, will you? But listen, I'm quite certain I gave them to Sinéad, and after all she has the pouch they came in. She's told me that."

"Yeah, but if she's sticking to her guns, this is going to get awkward. Let me ask you the hard question. Is there any chance that she might have pocketed them with a view to selling them on?"

"Absolutely not! God, Mick, you know Sinéad as well as I do. She's as straight as a die, you know she is," Lyons said.

"Sorry, but I had to ask, and I won't be the only one putting that question either. You do realise I'll have to tell the boss about this, and pretty soon."

"Gosh, I hadn't thought that far ahead. But listen, can you help me have a really good search of my office before we take this any further? They're only small, and they might have rolled into a crack somewhere," Lyons said.

"Yes, OK. But you should ask Sinéad to do the same, but be careful not to accuse her of anything. We just need to solve this little mystery and quickly. How's the case going anyway?"

"Don't ask. Can we go and do this now, Mick?"

"Yes, of course. Give me a minute just to send this email, then I'll be with you."

* * *

"What's going on with the super and Lyons?" Flynn said to Sally Fahy, as they saw the two senior officers going into Lyons' office looking anxious.

"God knows. But there must be something up. See if you can hear anything," Fahy said.

Flynn got as near to the door of Lyons' office as he dared without being seen, but he couldn't make out what was going on. There was no conversation, just the sound of them rummaging around inside the room. He looked back at Fahy and shrugged.

Inside the office, a thorough search was ongoing, but despite their best efforts, nothing of interest was discovered. When they had been crawling around on the floor for several minutes, looking under all the furniture and at the edges of the skirting board, they both stood up.

"They're not here, love. Are you sure Sinéad hasn't got them?" Hays said.

"No, she hasn't. I asked her several times, and she's adamant that they were on my desk when she left. I don't think she has them, honestly, Mick."

"Hmm... OK, well you know what happens next."

"Make my day," Lyons said with a grim face.

"I'll have to tell Plunkett. God knows what he'll do, but it will be a lot worse if we don't tell him," Hays said.

"Do you want me to do it?" she said a little plaintively.

"No, no. That's my job. And just to keep us right, you reported this to me formally, OK?"

"Yes, OK. I suppose I'd better get ahead of it a bit and write up a report too."

"Not a bad idea. But keep it to yourself until it's requested. There's still just a slim chance we might be able to handle it informally. I'll go up and see if he's around now. Best you don't go anywhere till we see which way the wind is blowing. All right?"

"Yes, I suppose so. But don't forget we still have a murder to solve," Lyons said.

"I hear ya. I'll let you know after I've seen him. And try not to worry too much, hun."

Lyons just smiled.

Chapter Thirteen

Lyons couldn't settle to anything after her partner had left the room. She sat at her desk, but could only fidget, and scan her computer screen without actually seeing any of the text that was on it. She lifted the phone to call Sinéad Loughran, but put the receiver back in its cradle halfway through dialling the number. She had no idea what to say.

She got up and went to the makeshift kitchen that was at the back of the office and put the kettle on to boil. As it started singing gently, Sally Fahy came in and joined her.

"Hi, boss," Fahy said.

Lyons looked up and acknowledged the junior officer, but said nothing. She busied herself rinsing two mugs under the cold tap and fetching down the jar of instant coffee.

"Is everything OK, boss?" Fahy said.

"Sorry, Sally, no, not really."

"What's up?"

Lyons wasn't sure if she should take Sally Fahy into her confidence, and tell her about the missing diamonds. But she was feeling very anxious about the situation and decided that she could trust Fahy implicitly. So, she shared the issue with her colleague, who was more of a friend really, and immediately felt better for it.

"Blooming heck! What does Superintendent Hays say about it?" Fahy said.

"He hasn't said much. At least he hasn't called me names. He's gone upstairs to fill Plunkett in."

Lyons poured the boiling water into the two mugs and handed one to Fahy.

"God, I'm sorry. But never mind. I'm sure it will be all fine. The stupid things can't be far away."

"You'd think so, wouldn't you. But we've had a really good look, and they've just, well, disappeared. I'd better get back to my office in case Mick calls. Catch you later."

"Is there anything I can do, boss?" Fahy said.

"No, thanks, Sally. It's my problem. I'll let you know how I get on."

Lyons walked slowly back to her office, glancing here and there as she entered the room in case the diamonds had mysteriously reappeared. But of course, they hadn't. She sat back down and sipped her hot coffee thoughtfully. It wasn't long before her thoughts were disturbed by her telephone ringing.

"Hi, it's me," Mick Hays said, "listen, could you meet me outside Plunkett's office. And bring Sinéad with you. He wants to talk to the three of us."

Lyons' stomach churned. But she considered the overall boss of the station to be a fair man, if a little stern at times. So, she didn't panic.

* * *

Lyons, Loughran and Hays stood outside Superintendent Finbarr Plunkett's office where his administrative assistant was guarding the entrance. Although she received no perceptible signal from within, she looked up from her keyboard and said, "You can go in now."

Hays knocked and entered the room. Plunkett was seated behind his spacious desk, which, for once, was cluttered with files and papers of all kinds.

"Come in, be seated. I'll be with you in a minute," the senior man said.

He continued to read a few sheets of paper and sign or initial them before turning them over and placing them in an ever-increasing pile, face down, at the edge of his desk. When he had completed four or five of them, he looked up.

"I have familiarized myself with the incident concerning the missing evidence, so there's no need for us to go back over that territory. As you know, the force takes these matters very seriously, especially where a major crime is involved," he said, folding his arms across his chest, "and the guidelines that I have now to follow are unambiguous. I've already been in contact with your manager, Ms Loughran. I'm afraid both you and Senior Inspector Lyons are suspended until further notice on full pay. Inspector, I need your warrant card please," he said, unfolding his arms and outstretching his hand.

Lyons thought quickly. Should she protest? Should she ask for more time, or attempt to negotiate? She looked at Hays for inspiration, but his face was totally expressionless. She reached into her jacket pocket and took out her wallet. She removed her warrant card and handed it across the desk to Plunkett's open hand.

"Thank you," he said, dropping the card into his desk drawer. "Now, I must ask you both to leave the station and not return until you hear directly from me. Is that clear?"

"Yes, sir. Will that be all?" Lyons said.

"Can I at least go back to my desk to collect my personal belongings?" Loughran interjected.

"That would be inadvisable. You could compromise your position further by doing so. I suggest you just leave. Your stuff will be perfectly safe," Plunkett said.

Hays caught Lyons' eye and indicated that she should go. He was going to remain behind with Plunkett for a few more minutes. The two women got up and left the room rather sullenly.

"C'mon, Sinéad," Lyons said, once they were outside, "let's go across the road and get a coffee or something stronger. This is bullshit!"

When they were seated in the café where they often drank coffee in happier times, Loughran said, "What now, Maureen?"

"Jesus, I don't know. I've never been in this position before. It's nuts. I'm not sure what to do. I'm not going home to watch Judge Judy on TV for two weeks, that's for sure!"

Before Loughran could reply, Lyons' phone burst into life.

"Hi, it's me. Can you talk?" Hays said.

"Yes. Listen, what the hell's going on, Mick?"

"Don't worry. It's not as bad as it seems. Plunkett is using the suspension to keep GCOS away from it. Once he's been seen to take action, they won't get involved for ages. He's cutting you loose. You can keep investigating this case, and both of you will be unfettered by protocol. You can use Sally and Eamon, but only contact them on their personal mobiles. I'll have a word with Mulholland too and give him the lowdown."

"Jesus, Mick! But what about the diamonds?" Lyons said.

"Don't worry about that for the moment. We'll keep looking for now, but if we find them, we might keep it quiet for a few days to give you some time to do your sleuthing. And don't worry about your HR record. This won't appear on it. I have his word on that, and I believe him," Hays said.

"Bloody hell! This thing gets more bizarre every minute. Are you sure about all this?" Lyons said.

"Yes, it's fine. Trust me. This is a good strategy. I suggest you get back out to Clifden as soon as you can and mingle with all those arty-farty types before the festival finishes and they all vanish. That's where the answer lies."

"Hmm... OK. Look, I'm going to go now. I need another coffee to process all this. Then we'll head out west. I'll call you later. Love you," Lyons said, and hung up.

Chapter Fourteen

It took Lyons and Loughran an hour and a half to go to both of their homes and pack a bag of appropriate clothing for what lay ahead. Then they were back on the road, heading west along the N59 through Moycullen and Oughterard, and on towards Maam Cross and Recess. It was still very bright, and the idyllic scenery calmed their anxiety a little as they crossed the boggy heathland, where the lakes on either side of the undulating road sparkled in the evening sunshine.

Neither of them was very talkative. They had too much to think about. Lyons pondered how things had got to such a state, and wondered if what her partner, Mick Hays, was telling her was entirely true. Loughran's mind was spinning. She was normally a happy-go-lucky type, gregarious and good humoured almost all of the time, even when attending a gruesome crime scene. But the events of the day had changed her. She was quiet and subdued, trying to resist the temptation to blame her travelling companion for her plight. She knew she had left the diamonds in Lyons' care.

But as they approached Clifden, Loughran said to Lyons, "Where are we going to stay?"

"I think the Alcock and Brown would be a good bet. Wasn't that the place that was on the business card we found?" Lyons said.

"Yes, I think so. Good idea."

When they arrived in Clifden, they pulled up outside the Alcock and Brown Hotel at the top of the town and parked Lyons' car. Taking their luggage in hand, they went inside and spoke to the girl on reception whose name was engraved on a badge on her lapel, identifying her as Julia.

"Hello, Julia," Lyons said, "we were wondering if you might have a couple of rooms available for us?"

Julia consulted a large ledger that was resting on the reception desk. Apparently, the hotel hadn't adopted an electronic reservations system as yet.

"How long will you be staying?" Julia asked.

"We're not sure. Two or three nights at least," Lyons said.

"Well, the festival crowd are starting to leave now, so I have two rooms at the front looking onto the street I could give you. Would that be all right?"

"Yes, perfect. Thanks. How much is it per night?" Lyons said.

"Do you want breakfast included?"

"Yes, please," Loughran said.

"That will be one hundred and twenty euro per night each, but if you stay three nights, you get an extra night at no cost. Have you a bank card?"

Lyons rummaged in her handbag and produced the card to complete the transaction, and the two women went upstairs to their adjacent rooms. As Lyons turned to enter her bedroom, she said, "When you've unpacked your toothbrush, come back, and we'll hatch a plan."

"Right. Give me five minutes," Loughran said, disappearing into her own room.

Lyons put her bag on the bed and went to the window. As Julia had said, the room looked out onto the street. The glass was clean, as were the net curtains that hung on the inside of it, but there was quite a lot of traffic and street noise coming in. "Never mind," Lyons thought out loud, "that will quieten down later."

After a few minutes there was a knock on her door, and Loughran came in. She sat on the edge of the bed.

"What now, Maureen? I really haven't a clue how this detecting thing works," Loughran said.

"Don't worry about it. Just follow my lead. Why don't we smarten ourselves up a bit and go down to the bar, see who is around? We might pick up some local gossip."

"OK. Give me ten minutes and I'll be ready."

* * *

A few minutes later the two of them were heading for the bar. Loughran looked stunning in a black halterneck sleeveless top with a cardigan and pale-coloured straight cut pants, her blonde hair loose to her shoulders and her bright blue eyes sparkling. Lyons was equally well turned out, in a summer print dress and sandals, also with a black cashmere cardigan just draped around her shoulders and her shiny dark brown hair. When they got downstairs to the lounge, it was quite busy. They went to the bar to order their drinks, and sat themselves up on two bar stools. It wasn't long before they drew some attention.

A young man in his late twenties who was sitting drinking with a few others of the same age approached the bar. He tried rather pathetically to chat up Lyons and Loughran, but they gave him short shrift, much to the amusement of his mates.

A few minutes later a tall man, in his late forties, Lyons guessed, came to the bar to order drinks. While the bartender was dispensing his libations, he started chatting to Loughran.

"Hi, my name is Vincent, Vincent Henderson," he said in a cultured British accent. He extended his hand to be shaken.

Loughran exchanged a quick, knowing glance with her colleague.

"Sinéad," Loughran said simply.

"Are you girls here for the festival?" the man continued.

"Yes. Just for a few days. And you?" Loughran said.

"Yes. I'm an art dealer. I go around to all these things. It's amazing what you can pick up if you have a good eye. The more remote the location, the less people know the value of what's on offer."

"I presume you mean the artwork and not the ladies you encounter," Loughran said, flirting mildly with him and smiling. He smiled back, but wasn't embarrassed by his *double entendre.*

"What are you after yourselves?" Henderson said, looking across to where Maureen Lyons was quietly sipping her drink.

"Oh, you know. Just on the lookout for anything interesting that crops up. A bit like you. But we mustn't keep you from your friends," Loughran said, noting that the man's drinks order was now fully prepared and sitting on the bar counter.

"Yes, of course. Maybe we will meet later on," he said coolly, and started to gather the various glasses into his hands.

"Maybe," Loughran said, and turned back to Lyons and started talking to her about nothing in particular. When Henderson had departed back to the far side of the lounge, well out of earshot, Lyons said, "That was a bit of good luck. And he seemed very keen on you!"

"A bit too keen for my liking, Maureen. And he wasn't giving much away either."

"No, I gathered that. Anyway, let's just hang around a bit longer and keep an eye on him. But to be honest, I'm quite tired. I wouldn't mind hitting the sack sometime soon, and I have to call Mick before I go to sleep," Lyons said.

They spent another hour or so over one more drink apiece, but no one else came near them, and the lounge was beginning to thin out. Henderson had left, although they didn't see him go, or where he went. So, they decided to call it a night. On the way back up to their rooms, Loughran asked, "What do you want to do tomorrow, Maureen?"

"I'd like to go down to the showgrounds and have a look at the last of the exhibitions before they pack up. We just might get some inspiration about what's going on out here."

"Do you want to check in with Sergeant Mulholland?" Loughran asked.

"No, better not. He knows we are here, but I don't want to put him in a difficult position unless it becomes absolutely necessary."

"OK. Well, here we are. I'll bid you goodnight. Sleep well," Loughran said, and went into her room, closing the door behind her.

When Maureen Lyons had changed into her pyjamas and dressing gown she lay down on the bed and phoned Mick Hays.

"Hello, you. How are you settling in?" Hays said when he answered.

"We're in the Alcock and Brown. Apart from being chatted up by some English dude at the bar, there's nothing happening here. We're going down to the showgrounds tomorrow morning to see if we can see anything. What about you, Mick?"

"I'm missing you, Maureen. And it's tricky trying to keep everyone on-side here, if you know what I mean. I don't want the idea that Sinéad and you are some pair of jewel thieves gathering momentum! But I think I'm ahead of the rumour mill, for now at least. Have you checked in with Sally or Eamon?"

"No, not yet. Do you think I should?"

"Well, perhaps not tonight, but it might be no harm to give one of them a call in the morning just to touch base. I had another word with Plunkett by the way. You won't have any trouble from him for a good while, unless of course you turn up in Hardy's trying to flog a couple of diamonds," Hays said.

"Ha ha. Very funny. But that's good to know anyway. I'm missing you too by the way. This feels weird. Anyway, I'd better see if I can get some sleep. I'll give you a ring tomorrow when we will hopefully have something to report," Lyons said.

"OK, love. Sleep tight. Kisses."

"Thanks, Mick. Kisses back to you. Goodnight."

Chapter Fifteen

Maureen Lyons was woken by noise coming in from the street. She squinted at her watch, and saw that it was 3:10 a.m. The street noise had died down at around midnight, and Lyons had fallen asleep soon after that. She eased herself out of bed and leaving her room in darkness, went to the window, drawing back the net curtain to look out. Down on the street there were two cars with their boots open, and Henderson was carrying something from one car to the other. The object was just short of a metre long, and was wrapped in cloth with tape around it. Once the item was placed in the boot of the receiving car, the two men stood on the footpath in some kind of earnest conversation that Lyons couldn't hear properly.

Lyons went to her night table and picked up her phone, dialling Loughran's number, hoping that her colleague would not have switched hers off for the night.

Loughran answered on the third ring.

"Hi, Sinéad, it's me. Listen, there's something going on outside that doesn't look right. Can you put some clothes on and meet me in the corridor?"

"Yes, sure. Two minutes."

Lyons pulled on a pair of jeans over her pyjamas, and put on a woolly jumper on her top half. She slipped on her flat shoes and left her room silently. Outside in the corridor she met Loughran just exiting too.

"C'mon. Let's see if there's a back way out of here, and be nice and quiet," Lyons whispered.

They tiptoed down the stairs, which fortunately didn't creak, and at the bottom, made their way towards the back of the building through a door marked 'Staff Only'. Following their instincts, they came to a door which looked like the fire exit from the kitchens. Hoping that it wasn't alarmed, Lyons pushed the door, and it yielded with a bit of a clank, but no alarm. They slipped out silently into the night and found themselves in a yard at the rear.

Lyons signalled to Loughran towards the exit, and a moment later they found themselves in Church Street which ran steeply uphill along the side of the hotel. They crept stealthily downhill towards the front of the hotel to see Vincent Henderson getting into a sleek Jaguar, while the man whom he had been talking to was already seated in an older Toyota preparing to leave.

Lyons was fortunate to find the keys of her own Volvo in her jeans pocket, and as Henderson's Jaguar pulled away from the kerb, herself and Loughran made their way hastily to where Lyons' car was parked.

Lyons set off at a brisk pace in her car with no lights on. She could see the rear lights of Henderson's Jaguar disappearing down along Seaview. Just after the Bank of Ireland, the road forked, and Henderson took the right-hand part that would lead him up onto the Sky Road. When he reached the junction of Church Hill and the Sky Road, Henderson turned left towards the Abbeyglen Castle.

The full moon provided enough light for Lyons to follow at a safe distance and avoid running off the road. Henderson was driving quite sedately in any case, which made things easier.

"I hope he's not going too far, Maureen. Where does this road lead to anyway?" Loughran said.

"It just goes around in a huge loop and then back onto the Westport Road eventually. But I have a feeling we won't be going that far."

The clouds scurrying across the bright, almost full, moon created short periods of brightness, but at other times, it was hard to see. Lyons kept the red rear lights of the big Jaguar just in sight to give her some help with the navigation along the twisty, boggy road.

"Did you manage to get the registration number of the car?" she asked Loughran.

"Yes. I made a note of it."

"OK. Well, here goes. This will be a good test of Sally Fahy's loyalty," Lyons said, smiling. She used the buttons on the Volvo's steering wheel to select Fahy's mobile number, and pressed 'call'. After seven rings, a sleepy voice came on the other end of the line.

"Hello. Who's this?"

"Hi, Sally. It's me, Maureen. Sorry to wake you at this ungodly hour, but I need you to do something for me."

Fahy sat up in her bed and reached for the notepad and pencil that she kept there.

"OK. What do you need?"

"I'm sorry about this. But I need you to go into the station. I have a car reg number here that I want you to check out. I need everything you can get on the registered owner, right across all our systems. I'll hand you to Sinéad. She's here beside me, and she has the number."

"Oh, OK," Fahy said. She wasn't entirely delighted with the errand she had been given. It was half past three in the morning, after all.

"Hi, Sally. It's Sinéad. The number is 192-C-94099, and it's a Jaguar or perhaps a Daimler. We're not close enough to see which. Have you got that?" Loughran said.

"Yes, 192-C-94099. Obviously, a Cork vehicle. I'll go in straight away. Who should I call when I have the information?" Fahy said.

"Better call me. Maureen may have to switch her phone off or put it on silent," Loughran said, looking across at Lyons, who nodded.

"OK. I'll get going. I'll be as quick as I can."

"Thanks, Sally. Good night, or should I say good morning."

* * *

The car that they were following drove on past a few bed and breakfast places, and then swung left onto the Lower Sky Road. Lyons pulled back a little for fear of being spotted.

"Where does this go?" Loughran asked.

"I think it eventually joins back up with the main Sky Road out near Kingstown at the very end of the peninsula. But as we've turned down here, I doubt if he will go all the way," Lyons said.

Almost immediately, the lead car slowed and turned up the narrow lane at the side of the old coastguard station. Lyons drove on past the impressive building and pulled into a gateway a little further along on the left.

"What's this place?" Loughran asked.

"It used to be a coastguard station, but it was taken over in 1922 and then burnt out during the Civil War. It was derelict for years, but eventually it was bought back by a local family and totally refurbished. I think it's a guest house and some kind of interpretive centre now."

"I wonder what our man is doing here at this hour?"

"Who knows, but I'm going to find out. You stay here and take Sally's call when it comes through. If I'm not back in an hour, send in the troops!" Lyons said, smiling.

"Be careful, Maureen, you don't know what you're getting into here," Loughran said.

"Don't worry, I'll be fine."

And with that, she got out of the car, having first switched off the interior light. As soon as she was out on the road in the cool morning breeze, she took out her phone and set it to silent.

Chapter Sixteen

Lyons crossed the road and walked back to the entrance of the coastguard station. She crouched down and went onto the grassy field in front of the building and headed to the right where she was able to creep up along the dry-stone wall that separated the land from the laneway that the Jaguar had taken. She crept up along the wall until she had passed the main building and found herself in a large, concreted yard with several sizeable outbuildings arranged in three sides of a rectangle facing the back of the coastguard station itself. The dark blue Jaguar was parked sideways across the yard, with its boot open, and Lyons could see that there was a light on in what appeared to be a stable block, although there was no sign of any livestock. She flattened herself against the wall as best she could, and edged slowly towards the entrance to the building that seemed to be occupied.

As she neared the door, she was able to glance in carefully through an adjacent opening. Inside the building, there was a series of shelves arranged along one wall. Most were bare, but on a shelf near the top, she saw a number of what looked like cast statuettes depicting traditionally dressed people from another era. The male figures had bockety hats and wizened faces, with suits hanging raggedly from their thin frames, while the women, also thin and emaciated in appearance, had scarves over their hair and shawls wrapped around. Some of them were holding small babies. Lyons assumed that these items were representations of Irish people during the famine years from the mid-nineteenth century.

Against the other wall there was a workbench with various tools spread around on it, and standing at the bench doing something with the base of one of the figurines was the man they had been talking to in the bar at the hotel earlier.

Lyons didn't want to get caught in this situation, so she quietly stepped backwards away from her observation point. Unfortunately, there was an old bucket that she hadn't seen behind her, and it went over with a loud rattle as it rolled away across the concrete. Lyons turned and ran as fast as she could back the way she had come. She glanced over her shoulder and saw the man in pursuit, but Lyons was fit, and fast, and she soon managed to increase the distance between herself and her pursuer. She got to the car, gasping for breath from the effort, jumped in, started the engine, and drove off at high speed, again with the lights off.

Loughran was taken totally by surprise by all of this, and as she was hurriedly fastening her seatbelt, she said, "Jesus, Maureen, what the hell happened?"

Lyons relayed the events that had taken place in the yard.

"We're not out of the woods yet, Sinéad. Yer man probably knows where this road leads, and he could easily head us off further along. Maybe we should pull in somewhere and lie low till it gets bright and then mingle in with the other traffic."

"No, there's no need. I've been studying the map while you were doing your James Bond impression. There's a track just up here a bit on the right that takes us all along behind the coastguard station. It comes out onto the N59 near the camping and caravan place. He'll never figure that out."

"Unless he stops and listens carefully. He'll hear the sound of our engine and he'll know what we're up to," Lyons said.

"It's a chance we'll have to take. Keep the revs low, but my guess is he'll go right past that track and on towards Kingstown and then he'll double back. We'll be safely tucked up in bed before he makes it back to Clifden!"

Lyons, with the help of Loughran, found the narrow lane that had been identified, and turned onto it. It was rough and bumpy, and Lyons had to concentrate hard to keep the car on course, twisting the steering wheel violently from time to time to avoid an enormous pothole. Weeds and brambles brushed against the sides of her Volvo making eerie squeaking noises as they progressed.

"God, I hope you're right about this track, Sinéad. It looks as if it could be the road to nowhere. I wish we had your big 4x4 for this job," Lyons said.

"Trust me, we'll be fine. When we get close to the N59, you can put your lights on. That'll make it easier."

After fifteen minutes of being bounced around on the rough surface, as predicted, the unmarked road intersected with the N59. Lyons turned right, back towards Clifden, hoping that her car hadn't been damaged by its passage across the rough terrain.

They got back into the town without further ado. Dawn was breaking, and they could see contrails high up in the early morning sky from the many aircraft that plied their way eastwards from the USA. Lyons pulled the car up to the kerb outside the hotel and switched off the engine.

"What now?" Loughran said.

"I'm too wired to get back to sleep, Sinéad, but you go back to bed if you like. I'm going to wait for Sally's phone call. And I have some thinking to do."

"Na, you're grand. I'll not sleep now either. I'll wait with you if that's OK?" Loughran said.

"Yes, of course. But listen, Sinéad, I can't really get you too involved in whatever is going on out here. You're not a cop, after all, and it wouldn't be fair to involve you if things get rough."

Loughran stayed silent for a moment.

"Well firstly, Maureen, I'm already up to my neck in this. Plunkett thinks I've nicked a few grands worth of jewels from the evidence locker, and anyway, you're not a cop just now either. So, let's stick together till we find out what the hell this is all about. OK?"

"Hmm... OK, if you're sure. But we are out on a bit of a limb here. Let's hope it doesn't get too messy. By the way, I think we should talk to Séan Mulholland at some stage today too. He needs to know what we are up to, and he may be helpful."

"Won't he be inclined to follow the force's protocols and treat us as if we have leprosy?"

"No, not Séan. We know each other better than that. We used to work together years ago when I was a sergeant, and we've stayed good mates ever since. We have a healthy respect for each other's methods, even though they can be very different," Lyons said.

"Oh, I didn't know. How will you contact him?"

"He usually goes for a walk up the town at around eleven in the mornings and stops in the little café beside the draper's shop for a cup of tea and a bun. We can just bump into him there."

"Sounds like a plan," Loughran said.

As they were wondering whether it was too early to go inside and find some breakfast, Lyons' phone sprang to life. She could see from the screen that it was Sally Fahy calling.

"Hi, Sally. Thanks for calling back. What have you got?" Lyons said.

"Hi, boss. I'm not finished yet, but I found out quite a bit about Henderson. I have his address, but that's not the interesting bit," the young officer said.

"Go on."

"Well, it looks as if he is some kind of business consultant. He has a registered business called Vincent Henderson and Company that operates out of a small office on Merrion Square in Dublin. He's registered with the Central Bank, and there's just one upheld complaint about him from a year ago. He was fined one thousand euro for failing to protect a client's data. But on Boards.ie there's more. Some bloke who calls himself 'HardDoneBy', all one word, says Henderson did him out of an inheritance of forty grand, but the posting is anonymous and there's no reply from Henderson," Fahy said.

"Are you sure it was the same Henderson, Sally?"

"From what I can see, it is, but I haven't finished checking around yet. I thought you should know in any case," Fahy said.

"Yes, you're right. Thanks, Sally. Look, can you keep looking for us?" Lyons said.

"Of course. How are you getting on, anyway?"

"Ah, ye know. I'm not sure what's going on really, but there's a lot not right about our Mr Henderson, that's for sure. Give me a call back when you have more, Sally, and thanks. I know this isn't easy for you."

"Ah, don't worry. It'll be fine. I'll call you later. Bye."

"Bye."

Chapter Seventeen

The autumn sun was bathing the main street in Clifden as Loughran and Lyons wandered down towards the café. The place was quite busy. It was the last day of the arts festival, so perhaps some extra visitors had come to the town hoping for a bargain, as exhibitors decided to part with their work at reduced prices rather than carry it all back home again.

The two women entered the little outlet, and spotted Sergeant Mulholland seated near the back. In front of him on the table was a teapot, a mug, and a small plate that was struggling to accommodate an enormous scone which was plastered with butter and jam and was partly devoured.

"Come in, ladies," Séan Mulholland said when he saw them, "sit ye down. What can I get you?"

Almost simultaneously, a short grey-haired woman in a flour-covered apron came out from behind the counter and stood by the table as Lyons and Loughran took their seats.

"Just a pot of tea for me, please, Séan," Lyons said.

"Same," echoed Loughran.

"Ah, now away with ye," Mulholland said. "You can't come in here without sampling one of Mrs Mulligan's home-made scones with that delicious raspberry jam that she makes herself too."

Seeing that Mrs Mulligan was looking expectantly at them both, Lyons responded, "Well, maybe just one between the two of us then, thanks very much."

When the woman had gone off to prepare their snack, Mulholland asked Lyons, "So, any news, Maureen?"

Lyons filled Mulholland in with all the information she had gleaned from her nocturnal expedition the previous night.

"That'll be the old workshops up behind the coastguard station. Am I right?"

"Yes. It looks like they were stables at one time, or something like that," Loughran said.

"Yes. There was a fella from around here that used to have a bit of a workshop up there. Wait a minute now, eh …. O'Rahilly, yes, that was it, Fergal O'Rahilly. But he hasn't been using it these last few years, as far as I know," Mulholland said.

"What did this O'Rahilly character do up there, Séan?" Lyons asked.

"A bit of welding, fixing up old bits of farm machinery that was nothing but scrap, really. And I think he dabbled a bit in cars at one stage too, but the coastguard people didn't like it, so they put a stop to it. It was making the place look like a scrap yard."

"Well, Henderson was up to something there last night. But I couldn't get in close enough to see what was going on. He's still here though. His big posh Jaguar is parked outside the hotel this morning. Have you found out anything more about the victim, Séan?"

"No, I'm afraid not. But I gave Eamon Flynn a call yesterday, and he said he was contacting the British police to see if they had anything of interest on any of the names yer man was going under. Anything more from the car?" Mulholland said, looking at Sinéad Loughran.

"I can't really contact anyone back at the lab. It would put them in an awkward position, what with me being suspended. But you could give Keith a call, Sergeant, if you have the time."

"Of course. I'll do that as soon as I get back to the station. What are you two going to do now?" Mulholland said, packing the last of his scone into his mouth and washing it down with the remains of his tea.

Lyons looked at her watch, and saw that it was coming up to noon.

"I think we'll go back down to the festival at the showgrounds. I've developed a sudden interest in small statuettes of old Irish people. Let's see if we can pick up a bargain!" Lyons said with a twinkle in her eye.

"You be careful now, lass. One tragedy in Clifden this week is enough for us to be going on with. Will you be around for the closing parade later on?"

"What does that entail?" Lyons asked.

"Once it gets dark, at about half past eight, there's a candle-light procession from the showgrounds up through the town to the monument. And then some dignitary or other makes a speech thanking all and sundry for a successful event and all the usual guff. The whole thing goes on for about an hour, and then said dignitary buys drinks for anyone who can fit into King's Bar. And then, ladies, the show is over, and Clifden returns to some form of normality for a few months, thank God."

"Any idea who is going to do the honours?" Loughran asked.

"No." Mulholland smiled. "They don't share that information with me, but it's usually one of the businessmen from the town, or if there's a member of the council or maybe even a real politician here, then he or she will be pressed into service."

"You're getting cynical in your old age, Séan," Lyons said, smiling.

"Not really. But I remember when this thing started. It was just a few paintings in the library and maybe in one or two of the shops. It was much less fuss then. Now the whole place is turned on its head for the duration, and look what we have to deal with. I'll be glad when it's finished and done with."

Lyons offered to pay for the refreshments when they had finished eating and drinking, but Mulholland wouldn't hear of it. He tendered a twenty-euro note to Mrs Mulligan, and she scurried off, returning briskly with what looked to Lyons to be almost the same amount in change. She smiled inwardly at the strange ways of rural Ireland.

"Will I be seeing you later?" Mulholland said, putting his peaked Garda cap back on his head as they stepped out of the building.

"Probably. But don't worry about us, Séan. We are well able to look after ourselves, and thanks for the tea and cakes," Lyons said.

Mulholland walked off in the direction of the Garda station, and Lyons said to Loughran, "Let's sit in my car. I want to call Eamon and see if he's found out anything about our victim. I think I'm beginning to get a feeling for what's going on here."

"Do tell. I'm totally lost," Loughran replied.

"All in good time, Sinéad."

* * *

"Hi, Eamon, it's me, Maureen. Can you talk?"

"Oh, hello Gráinne. Sorry, this isn't a good time. Can I call you back in a few minutes?"

"Yes, sure. Bye."

When she had finished the call, she said to Loughran, "Eamon was with someone. He called me Gráinne, so it must have been a bit awkward. He's going to call back shortly."

"Listen, Maureen, I'm getting a bit fed up with all this cloak-and-dagger stuff. We didn't do anything criminal after all. I'm thinking we should get back to Galway and see if we can't clear our names. The bloody diamonds must be somewhere. What do you think?"

"It's not that simple, Sinéad. Mick and Plunkett both know that we are still working on the case. The diamonds may even have been found by now, but it suits them to have us operating 'off piste' as it were."

"Well, any chance you could call Superintendent Hays and see what way the land lies? I'm getting quite nervous about our position."

"Yes, OK. But let's hear back from Eamon first, then I'll call Mick."

The minutes ticked by in silence as Lyons and Loughran sat in Lyons' Volvo. It was clear that Loughran was getting very fed up with the situation they had been placed in, and she wasn't put much at ease by her colleague's explanation and reassurances. Then Lyons' phone started ringing.

"Hi, boss. It's Eamon. Sorry about that, but there was someone with me."

"That's OK, Eamon, I got the message. Hang on while I put you on the speaker. Sinéad is here with me."

Lyons pressed the symbol on the screen in front of her, and Flynn's voice came through clearly inside the car.

"Hi, Inspector. How are things in the city?" Loughran said.

"Just peachy! We're missing the two of you, but the reason I rang back is that I have some information on our victim. Firstly, he seems to have switched between identities with consummate ease. In the UK, he's known mostly as Adam Dunne. He has a shop in a town near Aylesbury in England that sells antiques of sorts. He calls it 'Adamantiques' no spaces. It's some kind of a play on words, I think. He has come to the attention of Customs and Excise in the UK once or twice over restricted imports of one kind or another, largely from Africa, but they've never actually prosecuted him for anything."

"Wow! How did you manage to dig all that up, Eamon?" Lyons said.

"Ah, I have a contact in the Met in London who owes me a favour or nine, so he was glad to help out. He's going to do a bit more digging for me and let me know. I'm getting access to Dunne's bank account later on too, and that could tell us more. What are you two up to?"

"I have developed a sudden interest in small statues of poor Irish people modelled on what things were like during the famine. I'm going to the last day of the arts festival in a while to see if I can make a purchase. Sinéad will be my expert adviser," Lyons said looking at Loughran, who just grinned.

"OK. Well, mind how you go. I'll give you a bell later if I have anything more."

"Great, Eamon. Thanks."

Chapter Eighteen

The arts festival was reaching some sort of climax when Lyons and Loughran arrived at the showgrounds. The place was busy, and as expected the various stall holders were discounting their wares in an effort to avoid having to bring them home.

The two women strolled around feigning interest in several offerings, stopping here and there to fondle a piece of pottery, or standing back to study a painting or two. Some of the work was quite good, but nowhere near the standard of Paul Henry, who almost had a monopoly on Connemara landscape paintings. But the ambience was relaxing, helped by the Irish music playing in the background and the smell of freshly ground coffee coming from the catering stalls. Lyons' antennae were carefully tuned though, while Sinéad Loughran was just enjoying the rather aimless browsing.

Their meanderings brought them to a stand that had a number of figurines representing the poor of Ireland from the mid-nineteenth century. There were men, women, and even some very scrawny animals depicted in a kind of greeny-grey material, which made them look even poorer and more dejected than they would have been in real life.

There were about a dozen figures laid out along the front of the table belonging to the artist, each figure being approximately forty centimetres in height, apart from the animals which were proportionately smaller. At the back of the display, there was a box covered in green cloth upon which stood a much larger statue, measuring at least a metre high.

Lyons engaged with the stallholder.

"Hello. May I ask how much you are asking for the statues?"

"The figures are sixty-five euro each, but the animals are only forty. If you wanted one of each, I could do them both for one hundred," the man said.

Lyons lifted up one of the objects and stroked it gently, which she knew would be a buying signal to the vendor.

"What about that big one up on top?" Lyons said.

"I'm sorry," the man replied, "that's not for sale. It's a commissioned piece, and it's just here for display purposes."

"It's very impressive," Lyons said, smiling at the man, "could you take it down for me so that I can have a closer look? I might get one of those for my mam."

"I'm sorry, it's rather delicate. I can't let people handle it in case it gets damaged."

"Oh, I see. That's a pity. Do you have a business card so I can get in touch with you after the show if I want to place an order?"

The man reached into his jacket pocket and withdrew a small shiny gold case that was full of cards, removed one, and handed it to Lyons.

"Thanks. By the way, what would one of those cost in that size? Roughly, I mean?"

"Those, dear lady, are priceless! Give me a call after the show and we'll work something out for you. What's your own name?" he said.

"Gráinne. Gráinne O'Regan," Lyons said, drawing on the subterfuge used earlier by Eamon Flynn.

"Right, Gráinne. Don't forget now. Give me a call next week." With that the man turned his attention to another customer who was expressing genuine interest in some of his wares.

When they were out of earshot of the stall, Lyons said to Loughran, "Let's hang around for a bit. I get the feeling there's something dodgy about him and his precious statues. And I didn't like the way he wouldn't let me get close to the big one. Are you OK with that?"

"Yeah, sure. What's going on, do you think?"

"I don't know, Sinéad."

The two women continued to browse the various offerings while keeping watch on the stall that was selling the figurines. Loughran was drawn to a stand of abstract paintings in acrylic that seemed to capture the essence of the festival.

It wasn't difficult to mingle with the crowd, but sometimes they lost sight of their quarry for a few moments in the melee. Just before five o'clock when many of the stands had been cleaned out of merchandise, and even the coffee vendors were starting to pack up, Lyons glanced over to where they had been earlier. She noticed immediately that the large statue that was apparently so precious had gone. She nudged her colleague and nodded towards the stand in question.

"Did you see who took it, Sinéad?"

"No, sorry. I didn't."

"Let's get outside and see if we can spot anything," Lyons said. They pushed their way through the throng to the field outside and scanned the place thoroughly.

"There! Look, heading for the gate. It's that Henderson bloke. And he has something tucked under his arm wrapped in a towel or something," Loughran said, excitedly.

"Shit!" Lyons said. "I bet he has his car nearby, and ours is up at the hotel. C'mon. Let's get going. I bet I know where he's off to anyway with that thing."

They walked as quickly as they could back to their hotel and hopped into Lyons' car.

"Do you think we should alert Sergeant Mulholland, Maureen?"

"No. Remember, we're not supposed to be here on police business, and anyway, as far as we know Henderson may just have bought the statue for himself. It could be perfectly innocent," Lyons said.

"Do you really think so?"

"No, of course not. But this isn't the time to go off half-cocked. Let's just head out towards the old coastguard station and see what we can find."

Lyons turned the car and drove down through the town. She didn't want to be spotted by Henderson, so she decided to go the other way out to the Sky Road and approach the coastguard station from the Kingstown end. Twenty minutes later she brought the car to a halt in a gateway some 500 metres short of the lane that led up alongside the building.

"Will you stay here while I go and investigate, Sinéad?" Lyons said.

"No, I bloody won't. I'm coming too. We're in this together, whatever it is!"

They set off on foot, moving in a big circle through fields to avoid being seen by anyone looking out of the coastguard station, or from the buildings to its rear. As they climbed over yet another five-bar gate into a field with some black and white cattle grazing lazily on the meagre rations afforded by the late autumn grass, Loughran said, "Christ! I hope there are no bulls in this field. I can't run very fast in these shoes."

"Ah, you'll be grand. You'd be surprised how quickly you can sprint if you're being chased by one of those, but they don't seem too interested."

When they had completed a massive circle, allowing them to approach the outbuilding from behind, Lyons put her finger to her lips to indicate to Loughran to remain silent. They bent down and crept along by the back wall of the old stables, and came to a very grimy window that was splattered with mud and cobwebs. Lyons lifted her head so that she could peep into the building, hoping that whoever was inside wasn't looking out.

She was in luck. Inside, Vincent Henderson was standing with his back to the window at a work bench covered in tools of various kinds. The statue he had brought from the arts festival was laying on the bench on its back, and Henderson was cutting away at the base of the thing with an angle grinder. After a few moments, he turned off the noisy machine and pulled the base of the statue clear. He fumbled around inside the thing for a moment and then withdrew a small plastic bag. He opened the bag, and took out a black velvet pouch, just like the one that had originally held the diamonds that were found in Dunne's car. He tipped the pouch out on the bench, and despite the dirt of the window, and the distance between them, Lyons could clearly see the glistening sparkle of several stones which she assumed to be diamonds.

Lyons hunched down again, and signalled to Loughran to retreat. They went back the way they had come, and when they were a safe distance away from the old stables, Lyons told Loughran what she had seen. Back in their car, Loughran said, "Look, Maureen. We can't handle whatever is going on here on our own. We need to get back to town and get the others involved. I'm not a bit comfortable creeping around out here in the bog with diamond smugglers and possibly murderers as well."

"I think you're right. I'll give Mick a call."

Chapter Nineteen

"Hi, Mick. It's me. Have you got a minute?" Lyons said.

She was speaking from her car parked in a layby outside Clifden where there was a good phone signal.

"Yeah, sure. What's up?"

"It's a bit tricky, Mick. We're both getting very pissed off with this arrangement, and we've discovered something right iffy going on out here with that bloke Vincent Henderson. We need to get back in to follow this up. I can't handle it from outside the tent. What do you reckon?"

"Gosh," Hays said, "I don't know, love. It's a bit delicate. I suppose I could have another word with Plunkett, but he might not like it. He has spoken, as it were, and he won't like his authority being challenged."

"Christ, Mick, there must be something we can do. Sinéad hasn't even got her handbag with her. Plunkett wouldn't let her go back and get it when he booted us out," Lyons said.

"OK, look, give me an hour or so and I'll see if I can figure something out. Have you shared whatever you've discovered with the team back here?"

"No, but I'm expecting Eamon Flynn to call me a bit later. Please, try and sort this out for us, won't you? Clifden is lovely, but I don't want to be exiled out here forever, and anyway I'm missing you a lot," Lyons said.

"OK, don't worry, I'll figure something out."

Hays wasn't sure exactly what to do, but he decided to see if he could loosen out the situation a little. He called Keith Buckley, Loughran's loyal assistant at the forensic laboratory.

"Keith, it's Superintendent Hays here. Have you got a minute?" Hays said.

"Yes, of course, sir, how can I help?"

"I understand Sinéad Loughran's handbag and other personal effects are still there at the lab. She wasn't able to collect them when she was suspended, is that right?" Hays said.

"Yes. I put them in a locker and secured it. I have the key here."

"Good man. Listen, would you be prepared to retrieve that stuff and drive it out to my house in Salthill early tomorrow morning? I don't want to put you in an awkward position, but it's important."

"I suppose so. Do you mean unofficially?" Keith said.

"Yes, I'm afraid so. If you'd rather not, that's perfectly understandable."

"No, no that's fine. Sinéad is a good colleague. I'd like to help her if I can. Where is your place?"

Hays gave him the address and suggested that he should plan to be there before work, so as not to have an unaccounted absence.

"That's fine. I'll be there at about half past eight tomorrow, and I'll bring everything she's left here. There's her bag, a coat and scarf and a pair of gloves. Should I bring her laptop as well?" Keith said.

"Is it her personal property or does it belong to the job, Keith?"

"It's a work one, I think."

"Better not then. We don't want to get her into any more trouble. Just bring the personal stuff you described, and Keith, not a word to anyone, OK?"

"Yes, of course."

When Hays had finished the call, his administrative assistant buzzed him on the internal phone.

"Superintendent, when you were on the phone, you had a call from the UK. A Roger Watkins from the UK security services called. He asked if you could return his call," she said.

"Yes, thanks, Betty. Could you get him back on the line for me?"

"Yes, of course."

A few moments later, Hays' phone rang.

"Hays," he said.

"Oh, good afternoon. Is that Detective Superintendent Michael Hays?"

"Yes, this is he. May I ask who is calling?"

"My name is Security Agent Roger Watkins. I'm with MI5 here in London." The man had a well-educated south of England accent, and spoke quite slowly and deliberately.

"Hello, Mr Watkins. How may I help you?"

"I understand you are looking for information on a man that usually goes by the name of Adam Dunne. He's involved in the antiques and collectables business here in the UK. Your Inspector Flynn has been making enquiries."

"Ah, yes, I'm with you now. But why should that be of interest to MI5, Mr Watkins?" Hays said.

"What can you tell me of Dunne's whereabouts, Superintendent?" Watkins said, without answering the question. Hays recognised the tactic.

"Well, I know exactly where he is right now, but again I ask why that should be of interest to MI5?"

There was a silence on the other end of the line. Hays had the good sense not to punctuate it.

"Mr Dunne is a person of interest to us, Superintendent, and we'd very much like to be able to speak to him."

"I see. And may I ask why?"

The two men danced around each other for a few more exchanges. Hays was determined to let the MI5 man know that he wasn't speaking to a gobshite. Eventually, tiring of the duel, Hays coughed up.

"I'm afraid you won't be able to speak to Adam Dunne at all, Mr Watkins, you see, he is at present residing in our mortuary having been murdered recently at the Clifden Arts Festival."

"I see. That's most unfortunate. Have you apprehended the culprit at all?" Watkins said.

"Our investigation of the matter is still underway. We have a number of officers working on the case, but may I ask again, what is your interest?"

Watkins again went silent, and Hays waited patiently for the man to speak.

"This is highly confidential, Superintendent. If this gets out it could jeopardize months and months of tedious and complicated work across several countries. Do I have your word that what I'm about to tell you will be kept in confidence?"

"Mr Watkins, if what you have to tell me will help me to solve the crime we are investigating, then I'm afraid I can give no such guarantee. What I will say, is that we would be pleased to co-operate with you and your organisation to the fullest extent in whatever matters are of mutual interest, and it sounds to me as if there may well be a good deal of common ground tied up with Mr Dunne's demise. The very fact that we are having this conversation implies as much."

Watkins thought again for a moment.

"Very well, Superintendent. Mr Dunne was working for us. Not in any salaried position, you understand, but as an independent agent, undercover."

"I see. And now he's gone and got himself killed in my jurisdiction. I can see how that might be a tad awkward for you, all right. What was the nature of his work for you?" Hays said.

"He was trying – quite successfully as it happens – to penetrate a group who are dealing in conflict diamonds. We don't believe the gang are actually terrorists, but the profits, or some of them, from their endeavours may well be finding their way back to some pretty nasty types. May I ask what stage your investigation is at? Do you have any suspects as yet?"

"I'm not totally up to speed on the exact progress of the case, Mr Watkins. One of my senior inspectors is the SIO, and she's spending time out near the scene of the crime at the moment to gather evidence. Do you have any idea who may have been involved in Dunne's death?"

"Perhaps," Watkins said. "But not over the phone. Listen. I'm due a few days leave just now. I've often wanted to visit the west of Ireland in any case. I hear it's quite beautiful. Do you think if I came out there, we could meet up, and maybe have a chat with your SIO as well? It would be all completely off the record of course. I'd just be a holidaymaker."

"I don't see why not. Do you think you could find your way to Galway all right?" Hays said.

"I think I should be able to manage that. Why don't you give me your personal mobile number and I'll call you in a day or two when I arrive?"

Hays did as he was asked, and concluded the call.

Chapter Twenty

Hays called Lyons back as soon as he had finished with the man from MI5.

"Hi, can you talk? There have been some developments," he said.

"Yes, sure. What's up?"

Hays told his partner about the call from MI5, and the arrangements he had made for Keith to bring Loughran's personal belongings to their house in Salthill the following morning.

"I think you should drive back home tonight. Sinéad can stay at ours again, and I think with this new information, we may be able to get your suspensions lifted. I'll have a word with himself and see what way he's thinking."

"OK. That would be great. We'll leave shortly, and see you in about an hour."

"Great. See you then. I'll get a meal ready."

When the call was ended, Lyons told Loughran what had transpired.

"God, Maureen, that man of yours is amazing. Don't suppose I could borrow him for a few years – you know, just till we've had several kids and before I get old and wrinkly!"

"Hands off, girl. Don't even think about it! He's mine, all mine," Lyons said rolling her hands together like some demented witch.

"Ah well, worth a try, I guess."

The two women checked out of the hotel and put their cases in the boot of Lyons' Volvo. They drove back to Galway on their well-worn route. The setting sun had painted the clouds in glorious shades of pink and orange, and the stillness of the evening air gave a surreal appearance to the heathland as they progressed across the bog. They drove on through Recess, Maam Cross and on into Oughterard, Rosscahill and Moycullen before they hit the outskirts of the city. The traffic was busier than they expected, but they got to Lyons' house in Salthill within the hour as promised, and were welcomed by Hays and a delicious aroma of garlic, herbs and roasting beef.

* * *

Keith Buckley arrived at Lyons' and Hays' house as expected at quarter to nine the following morning. He rang the bell, and the door was answered by Sinéad Loughran who had been up for some time, and had cooked breakfast of bacon and scrambled eggs for her hosts.

"Ah, Keith, come in. Thanks a million," Loughran said, taking some of the items from Keith who was laden down with her stuff, "but I hope no one saw you carrying my handbag. People will talk, you know." She smiled broadly.

Keith had a quick look around in case his colleague was being serious, but there didn't seem to be anyone watching at that early hour. The people of the west of Ireland were sometimes accused of being lazy, as they tended not to rise very early in the morning. But this is easily explained. Galway is several degrees of longitude west of Greenwich. And although it keeps the same time as London and the rest of Ireland, the sun actually rises some forty minutes later in Galway than it does at Greenwich. So, it's little wonder that the people of the west are sometimes judged, unfairly, to be a bit fond of their beds. And they make up for it at the other end of the day when they are still carousing long after most Londoners have gone to sleep.

Keith followed Loughran into the kitchen where Hays and Lyons were still seated at the table.

"Hi, Keith. Thanks for this. Can we get you a coffee or a spot of breakfast?" Hays said.

"Coffee would be great, thanks, sir."

"It's Mick when we're at home, Keith, and Maureen," he said, nodding towards Lyons.

Lyons got up to see to Keith's drink. To free up space, Lyons lifted up Loughran's large blue leather handbag, which was more like a satchel than anything else. To say that it was capacious would be an understatement. And it was heavy – very heavy.

"God, Sinéad, what the hell have you got in here? It weighs a ton," Lyons said.

"I know. I must clean it out. Give it here," she said reaching for the bag. Loughran went to a vacant area of the kitchen worktop and tipped the bag out. All sorts of miscellaneous stuff tumbled onto the polished granite. Coins rolled around, and settled on the hard stone. Loughran shook the bag to get the last of the contents out, and as she did so, two small diamonds fell onto the worktop and came to rest just short of the edge.

"Shit!" Loughran shouted, causing the other three to turn and look at her.

Lyons realized what had happened, and went across to Loughran and put her arm around her.

"It's OK, Sinéad. Don't worry. Here, give me the bag."

Loughran handed it over, still in shock from what it had contained.

Lyons took the bag, and put her hand deep inside. She felt around in the bottom of it. "The lining is torn," she exclaimed. "They must have fallen down and got in behind the cloth, and they are so small, they got caught in the seams of the leather."

"Well, at least we have them back now. For heaven's sake, put them into a bag and seal it. Keith can take them back to the evidence safe," Hays said, finding it a little difficult to conceal his frustration.

"God, Maureen, I'm really sorry," Loughran said, a few tears forming in her eyes.

"Ah, look, don't beat yourself up. We have them back, that's what's important. And we've done some good work while we were pariahs too!"

Lyons poured out Keith's coffee and handed it to him.

"Thanks, eh... Maureen," he said, not entirely comfortable with using her first name. "By the way, there's a bit more too. You know that little yellow plastic thing that we discovered out at the showgrounds near yer man's body? Well, I've found out a bit more about it."

All eyes turned to Keith.

"Yes. I magnified the numbers etched into the side of it, and traced it back to the manufacturers. It came off a small fire extinguisher. It's the kind that is sometimes used on a boat or in a car. They're made in India, and distributed in the UK. I'm still trying to find out if any of them are sold in Ireland. They have to get back to me. Oh, and they are filled with nitrogen."

"That's great, Keith, well done you," Loughran said.

"Have you heard anything more from that crowd in England, Mick?" Lyons said.

"No. He's threatening to come over for a few days. It's all unofficial of course, so he's pretending to be on holiday. I'm not sure when he'll pop up. He likes to play things close to his chest. I had quite a job getting him to open up at all," Hays said.

"No better man," Lyons said, resting her hand on her partner's shoulder.

"Right, well I'd better talk to Plunkett and see if he's happy to rehabilitate you two now that the diamonds have been found again. Keith, if you could follow up on that fire extinguisher thing for us, that would be great. Oh, and please make sure the evidence is secured back at the station – properly this time," Hays said, looking at Lyons with a sly smile. "Now, I'm going into the front room to see if I can talk Plunkett around."

Hays got through to his boss surprisingly quickly.

"Good morning, sir. I just want to bring you up to speed on the evidence in this murder case out at Clifden that went missing."

Hays went on to tell the superintendent that the diamonds had been recovered, without going into too much detail about the fact that they had been hiding in the lining of Loughran's handbag all along.

"And are you certain, Mick, that we have this evidence secured now, and there won't be any further issues?" Plunkett said.

"Yes, sir. I'm sure."

"Right, so. On your head be it. I'll send Lyons' warrant card down to her office in a while. I take it she'll be back in at, say, ten o'clock?"

"Yes, sir. I'll make sure she is. And thanks, sir."

"Ah, you're grand. I don't think the story got out in any case. We'd look like right eejits if that became widely known. Are we making progress with the case?" Plunkett said.

"Yes, sir. Lyons and Loughran were busy out in Clifden, and there's quite a bit of new information coming through. And I'm keeping a bit of an eye on things too."

"Good man, Mick. That's the style."

Chapter Twenty-one

When Lyons got to the Garda station in Mill Street, she wasted no time in getting down to business. She summoned Sally Fahy and Eamon Flynn into her office.

"Right, folks, I want to go over everything we know about this case and see if we can progress matters. There's quite a bit of new information that has come to light. Why don't you both grab a coffee, and get me one too, and we'll make a start."

Eamon Flynn left the room to see to their drinks.

"It's good to have you back, boss. We were a bit all at sea here without you," Fahy said.

"Thanks, Sally. It's good to know I'm indispensable. But Superintendent Hays had my back in any case. I don't think I was in any real danger of being booted out."

"So, what's the story on yer man in Clifden then?"

"Hang on till Eamon gets back and then all will be revealed," Lyons said.

A few moments later, Eamon Flynn reappeared with three mugs of hot coffee and set two of them down in front of Fahy and Lyons.

"Thanks, Eamon. OK, well this is what we know. Adam Dunne, cleverly disguised as some sort of dealer, was actually working for MI5, the British security outfit. We'll know more soon. There's someone from there coming over to talk to Mick. But we can assume that Dunne had infiltrated some sort of international smuggling ring, and I guess someone must have discovered who he really was, and taken him out. Vincent Henderson is somehow involved too, but to what extent we don't know; for now at least," Lyons said.

"Yes, but what about the diamonds we found in Dunne's car? Do you think he was skimming as well? It looks a bit like that," Flynn said.

"Possibly," Lyons said. "Or maybe they were just the proceeds of some deal or other and he was keeping them as evidence."

"What about Dunne's mobile phone?" Fahy asked.

"Cripes, I'd forgotten about that, and with Sinéad out of action as well, I don't suppose anything has happened. Sally, can you give her a call when we're finished here and let's get moving on it," Lyons said.

"Yes, sure, boss. But I think it's fair to assume that the gang will probably go to ground for a while now after this. They'll be in damage limitation mode for a while, so it's going to be very hard to flush them out," Fahy said.

"You could be right, Sally. But we still have one string to our bow," Lyons said.

"What's that?"

"Henderson. He doesn't know I'm a cop. He chatted Sinéad and me up in the bar of the Alcock and Brown, but he didn't get a look at us later when we were out at the coastguard station, at least I don't think so. Maybe we could use that to our advantage."

"Hm... sounds a bit dodgy, boss. What have you in mind?" Fahy said.

"Nothing yet. But he's our only solid lead, and he definitely has something to hide."

"Why don't we do a raid on the workshop out on the Sky Road and see what we find? We should be able to tie him back to whatever he was doing there with fingerprint and other forensic evidence," Flynn said.

"I was thinking of something a bit more subtle than that, Eamon. Don't put anything in motion yet. I'll get back to you. Now, what about the evidence Keith has discovered from the little yellow plastic thing? Has anyone followed up on that?"

"No, boss. Sorry," Flynn said.

"Right, Eamon. Get whatever information Keith has. Then get onto the distributor in England and see if they sell any of those things in this country, and if so, to whom. Follow your nose to see if you can identify whoever bought the thing. I know it's a long shot, but it's about all we've got."

"Right, boss. I'll call Keith as soon as we're done," Flynn said.

When the meeting was over, Fahy and Flynn left Lyons in her office. It was clear to them that she had some thinking to do, and they had their assigned tasks.

Fahy spoke to Loughran about Dunne's mobile phone, and she agreed to drop over with it. When he had got hold of it, she approached John O'Connor – the detectives' unofficial technical wizard, who loved exploring phones, laptops and other electronic gizmos that they encountered during their investigations.

Fahy handed the phone to O'Connor.

"John, can you get me chapter and verse on this thing? I need the full monty. Call list in and out for the past three months; name and address of the subscriber; bank details for same, and if you can track its movement by location in the days before the owner was killed, all the better. OK?" Fahy said.

"Yes, sure. Leave it with me," O'Connor said, eyeing the device in anticipation.

"Thanks. Let me know when you have something."

* * *

Lyons had been brooding in her office for nearly an hour, plotting their next move. She lifted the phone, and called upstairs to Mick Hays.

Fifteen minutes later, she was seated in front of her partner in his large, comfortable office.

"So, what's on your mind, Maureen?"

Lyons went on to outline her plan to the superintendent.

"Crikey, Maureen, don't you think that's a bit risky, even for you?" Hays said.

"I can't think of any other way to move this forward, Mick. So far, we have very little evidence and very few leads. And I'd have Sinéad with me, so I think we'd be perfectly safe."

"Could you wait until I've had a chat with this bloke from the UK? He may give us more of an insight into what's going on," Hays said.

"If you think I should, Mick. But all the while the trail is going cold, and I'm not having some bloody gangsters coming onto my patch and screwing around thinking they can get away with it."

"God, you're gas, Maureen. OK, but I'm not telling Plunkett about it. I will make a few calls to ease your way a bit. When do you want to start?"

"Tomorrow."

Chapter Twenty-two

Merrion Square is one of three similar parks on the southside of Dublin. It was created towards the end of the eighteenth century when the Earl of Kildare built his magnificent residence nearby, known as Leinster House. Leinster House is now the preserve of the Irish Government, but in the eighteenth century it was a private house. Its presence encouraged the well-to-do of Dublin to move nearby, and so a number of squares of terraced Georgian houses were constructed, of which Merrion Square is but one. The houses had no front gardens, as the style at the time was for them to open directly onto the footpath, usually down a flight of granite steps. So, to provide green recreational areas for the residents, the squares were built, and at that time, access to them was permitted only to the residents of the surrounding houses.

These days, the very grand houses are given over to offices, and the green spaces have been opened to the public, providing welcome relief from the incessant hustle and bustle of the city going on all around them. Some of the offices are small, occupying just one or two rooms, while others are comprised of two or more of the properties joined together and remodelled internally. As offices, they are somewhat inefficient, but the grandeur of the houses themselves, with their high ceilings, ornate cornices, panelled doors, and gently inclined staircases with mahogany handrails, gives the spaces an air of opulence not readily enjoyed by modern 'brass and glass' buildings. As a consequence, the properties are usually occupied by what is described as 'professional undertakings', such as solicitors, financial advisors and medical professionals. It was in one of these places that the business of Vincent Henderson was located. For anyone that was interested, a brass plate bearing the man's name was affixed to the brickwork adjacent to the front door, itself painted an understated dark blue. The plate was polished, in contrast to some of the others which had been tarnished by the frequent rain.

Lyons had done two complete circuits of Merrion Square before she found a parking space on the side of the square where Henderson's offices were located. She manoeuvred her Volvo into the narrow space, placing the back of the car at ninety degrees to the kerb.

"I suppose we'll have to buy a ticket," she said to her companion. "Can you go and see if you can find a machine or something? Have you any coins, Sinéad?"

"Somewhere, in this sack I laughingly call a handbag, along with a few more diamonds that are still rolling around in the lining," she quipped. Lyons was hardly amused.

Loughran eased herself out of the car with some difficulty, trying not to hit the door against the adjacent vehicle. Five minutes later she was back holding up a small white printed ticket triumphantly.

"Blooming hell! This cost me nine euro, and it only lasts for an hour and a half. And the damn thing owes me a euro change to boot. Cheeky buggers!"

She sat back into the car and placed the ticket on the dashboard where it could be seen by any eagle-eyed parking warden.

"What do we do now?" Loughran said.

"Now, we wait. You may have spotted Henderson's Jaguar parked at the other end of this street. So, he's probably in his office."

Lyons consulted her watch. It was twenty past twelve.

"I'm guessing Henderson goes to lunch sometime between now and one o'clock. We'll follow at a discreet distance, and pop up in whatever wildly expensive bistro he's dining it. After that, we play it by ear. We'll pretend we have come to Dublin to see if we can buy you an engagement ring. You OK with that?" Lyons said.

"Chance would be a fine thing. But, yeah, sounds workable."

They didn't have long to wait. At twelve thirty-five, Henderson appeared at the door of his office. He was dressed in a well-cut business suit, smart shirt and tie, and shiny, black, lace-up shoes. He carried a lightweight, pale raincoat over his arm. He descended the steps of the building and took off, walking away from where the two women were parked. They scrambled out of Lyons' Volvo and followed at a discreet distance. Lyons was well used to following people without being seen, and Loughran fell into step alongside her.

At the corner of Merrion Square and Upper Merrion Street, Henderson turned left and walked up towards the junction of Ely Place. When he had passed The Merrion Hotel, opposite Leinster House, he disappeared down a set of steps into a restaurant that occupied the basement of number twenty. Lyons waited a few minutes with her colleague out on the footpath, pretending to be tourists admiring the impressive edifice opposite, and then followed down the stairs and into the restaurant.

The place was very tastefully decorated in a modern style. The walls had been taken back to the stonework, and small black tables with bulbous orange lights suspended overhead gave it a cavern-like feeling, but it was warm, and the girl at the desk just inside the door was welcoming.

The restaurant had just a few tables occupied. Lyons calculated that they had beaten the lunchtime rush by arriving early.

"Could you take two more for lunch?" Lyons asked the waitress who was smartly dressed in a well-pressed white blouse and black trousers.

"Yes, of course, take a seat anywhere," the girl said, handing them two large, laminated menus.

Lyons had spotted Henderson seated with his back to the wall about halfway down the floor, and she navigated herself and Loughran to a table close by, but not exactly adjacent to their quarry. They sat so that they could see Henderson, who had a newspaper folded in four and propped up against the water pitcher on his table. When the waiter brought Henderson's starter, which looked like a bowl of home-made vegetable soup, he put away his newspaper and turned his attention to the food. Lyons decided that this was her moment, and nudged Loughran on the arm, and emitted a loud cackle, as if some hilarious joke had been exchanged between the pair. Henderson looked up from his meal and recognised the women from their encounter in the Alcock and Brown Hotel previously. He called across to them.

"Gracious! You two must be stalking me, or is this just a coincidence?"

"Oh, hello. Fancy meeting you here," Lyons said across the void.

"Well, now that you're here, would you care to join me?" Henderson said.

"That would be very nice, but we're paying for ourselves, OK?"

"Whatever," he replied.

The waitress, who had been observing the exchange, quickly arrived to shunt two of the small tables together, move the menus onto the new location, and rearrange the cutlery and glassware.

"So, what are you doing here, ladies?" Henderson said when they were all resettled.

"Shopping, of course," Loughran said, smiling.

"Of course. But there aren't any shops around here. How come you ended up in this place?"

"Parking and sustenance for what lies ahead. After our drive from Galway, we're famished, and we're going to attack Grafton Street later which can't be done on an empty stomach," Loughran said.

The waitress came and interrupted the conversation taking the order for food from Lyons and Loughran. When she had gone off towards the kitchens, Henderson resumed the questioning.

"And is there something specific you've driven all this way to buy?" he said, looking at Lyons.

"Well, don't tell anyone," she said, lowering her voice, and leaning in a little towards the man, "but Sinéad here is getting engaged, and we're in town to see if we can find a nice big diamond engagement ring for her fiancé to buy for her. The selection in Galway isn't great, so we were thinking maybe Weirs would be the place to go."

Henderson took another mouthful of his lunch and dabbed his mouth with his napkin. "But surely the lucky man needs to be here. Where have you hidden him?" he said.

"Fintan travels a lot for work. Right now, he's in Asia doing something or other. And anyway, we won't actually *buy* the ring if we see one we like. Maybe just put a deposit down until he gets a chance to see it, and of course, pay for it!" Loughran said.

"What's it got to do with him, anyway?" Lyons said, giggling a little. "He's just your banker, Sinéad."

"God, that's a terrible thing to say, Maureen. You know I love Fintan. But you're right. He his rather well heeled," Loughran said smiling broadly.

"You know, if you go to Weirs, you'll be paying top dollar for anything decent they have in stock. And the margin on engagement rings is eye watering. You'd do much better to buy the stone yourself in the trade, and have it made into a ring by a proper jeweller. I reckon you'd save about half, or get a much more expensive ring for the same money."

Chapter Twenty-three

As the meal progressed, Lyons observed that Henderson deftly steered the conversation back onto the theme of jewellery, and diamonds in particular.

"What sort of budget have you got, Sinéad, for your ring?" he asked as the waitress took away their dessert plates and replaced them with coffee.

"Fintan said I could go up to eight thousand euro, or if I saw something I really wanted that was a bit more, that would be OK too," Loughran said.

"You'd get a really fine stone for that money in the wholesale market, I can tell you," Henderson responded, "and it will only cost you a couple of hundred to have it made into a ring. Do you prefer white gold or yellow gold?"

"Oh, yellow gold every time for me."

As they finished their drink, the waitress brought the bill and gave it to Henderson on a small chromium platter.

"We're splitting this three ways, right?" Lyons said.

"Oh, please ladies, let me. I don't often get to spend my lunchtime with two gorgeous women, and it's been fun finding out about your mission here in Dublin."

Henderson dropped his bank card on top of the bill and the waitress returned with a hand-held machine to complete the transaction. As Henderson was folding the receipt into his wallet, he smiled at the two women. "Tell you what. Why don't you let me drive you out to a friend of mine who deals in diamonds and let you have a look at what he has in stock? Weirs will still be there if you don't see anything you fancy, but it could save you, or Fintan, a pile."

Lyons spoke up before her colleague could reply.

"That would be terrific, but surely you have other things you should be doing this afternoon?"

"Nothing that can't wait for an hour or two. It's not far anyway," he said, standing up and collecting his raincoat.

The trio made their way back out onto Merrion Street, and started walking in the direction of Henderson's office on the square. As they approached his Jaguar, Henderson stopped. "Would you mind awfully if we took two cars? I can scoot off home after I've made the introductions. It will save me coming back into town."

"Yes, of course. This is very kind of you, Mr Henderson," Loughran said.

"Call me Vincent. Listen, why don't you come with me in my car, Sinéad, and you can follow on behind, Maureen?"

"Yes. OK. But don't drive too fast. I don't know my way around Dublin very well. What address are we going to in case I get lost?" Lyons said.

"Ah, don't worry. I'll keep an eye on you in my rear-view mirror, and it's not far."

Henderson and Loughran got into the Jaguar, while Lyons walked on down the street to retrieve her Volvo. She sat in, started the engine, and as she was fastening her seat belt, Henderson's sleek machine slid by in front of her. She pulled out of the parking space and fell in behind Henderson who was stopped at the corner of Merrion Square at the traffic lights. He waved to Lyons in his mirror, indicating that contact had been established. When the light went green, Henderson took off briskly into Upper Mount Street, heading for the Pepper Canister Church. He went past a white Nissan that was attempting to parallel park, but due to oncoming traffic, Lyons had to pull in behind the Nissan and wait. Henderson swung left in front of the church and disappeared out of sight.

As soon as she was able, Lyons pulled out around the Nissan that was having some difficulty squeezing into a space that was barely big enough for it, and set off in pursuit of her friend. But when she had rounded the church and come to the junction of Mount Street Crescent and the canal, there was no sign of the big car anywhere. Lyons crossed over Huband Bridge and turned right onto Percy Place. She accelerated quickly till she came to the junction of Haddington Road, looking everywhere for any sign of Henderson's car, but there was none. She instinctively turned right and was stopped by traffic at Baggot Street. Trying not to panic, when the traffic cleared, she drove across onto Mespil Road and pulled in just beyond the taxi rank.

Lyons took out her mobile phone and called Loughran's number, but it went through to voicemail without being answered. She tried to calm herself down by saying that Henderson had just moved on without checking that she was following, but she couldn't convince herself.

* * *

"I don't see Maureen's car behind us, Vincent. Maybe we should stop and wait for her," Loughran said.

"No, I can see her. She's about four cars back. She'll be fine," he said, accelerating away rather too quickly. By this time, Henderson was a long way ahead of Lyons on Grove Road, travelling west along the Grand Canal.

"I think I'll just give her a call on her mobile, just to make sure," Loughran said. But as she took her phone out of her handbag and powered it up, Henderson reached across and grabbed the instrument and threw it out of the driver's side window onto the road.

Loughran tried to remain calm. There was nothing to be gained at this stage by having a tantrum. "What's going on, Vincent?" she said as coolly as she could manage. "Where are you taking me?"

Henderson didn't reply. He made sure that the car didn't slow down enough to allow Loughran to jump out, even crashing a red light at one of the canal bridges to keep momentum. At Dolphin's Barn, Henderson swung left and then immediately right into a narrow lane. At the end of the lane he drove through tall green gates into a yard surrounded by single-storey buildings of various kinds and stopped on the broken concrete surface. He leapt out of the car, ran to the passenger's side, and yanked open the door.

"Out!" he said.

Henderson manhandled Loughran roughly towards a door in one of the low buildings, opened it, and thrust her inside. She stumbled, and fell to the rough floor, twisting her ankle in the process. Henderson went to a cupboard and took out some blue nylon rope and a roll of silver duct tape. Loughran tried to lash out at the man with her good leg, but the incapacity of her twisted ankle prevented her from landing a debilitating blow. Henderson tied Loughran's hands tightly behind her back, bound her feet together, and placed a piece of tape across her mouth. Loughran wriggled and grunted as much as she could, but it was no use, she was unable to help herself in any way at all.

Chapter Twenty-four

"Is that Superintendent Hays?" the man asked when Hays answered the phone in his office.

"Yes. Who's calling please?" he said, not immediately recognising the voice.

"It's Roger Watkins, Superintendent. I'm here in the lobby of the Imperial Hotel. I was wondering if this would be a convenient time for us to have a chat?"

"Oh, hello, Mr Watkins. Yes, this isn't a bad time. Do you want to come around to Mill Street?"

"I'd prefer if we met here, if that would be OK with you," Watkins said.

"Oh, yes, right. I'll walk around now. I should be with you in about ten minutes."

"Thanks. See you then." The line went dead.

As Hays walked around from the Garda station at Mill Street, crossing the Corrib River into Lombard Street and then through the narrower streets towards Eyre Square, he wondered how Watkins had avoided the alert that he had set up on the man's movements in and out of the country since they last spoke.

Hays arrived at the hotel just about ten minutes after he had spoken to Watkins. He entered the lobby, and immediately spotted the man sitting in an easy chair beside the open fire with a copy of *The Daily Telegraph* by his side. Watkins was unremarkable in every respect. He was of average height and build, with the kind of face that you could pass a hundred times in the street without even noticing. His dark brown hair, going a little grey at the sides, was conventionally fashioned, and his dress was as unremarkable as the man himself. He wore navy trousers, a pale blue button-down shirt, a tweed sports jacket of indeterminate hue, and polished black slip-on leather shoes. As Hays approached, Watkins stood up and extended his hand to be shaken.

"Mr Hays," he said, "nice to meet you. Can I get you a coffee or something?"

"Hello, Mr Watkins. Have you been here long?" Hays said, more for something to say as opposed to a genuine enquiry.

"About an hour. I was driven down from the JHC this morning."

"JHC?" Hays said.

"Sorry, yes, the Joint Helicopter Command base at Aldergrove in the North. I flew in first thing."

"Oh, right. Well, shall we sit?" Hays said, realising that Watkins was some sort of protected species within the British Security Services. The two men sat in the window of the spacious lobby, happy that they couldn't be easily overheard.

"So, what can you tell me about this business out at the Clifden Arts Festival?" Hays asked.

"Not very much, I'm afraid. It's part of an ongoing operation, so everything is on a need-to-know basis, as it were. I was wondering what you and your people have managed to make of it so far."

Hays recognised the tactic, and wondered if he was going to have another verbal game of cat and mouse with this Englishman. He decided to cut to the chase.

"Look, Mr Watkins, we can dance around each other all day if you want to, but I'd much prefer if we could be open with each other. We'll make much more progress, and I won't get pissed off nearly so quickly," Hays said, looking intently at Watkins.

Watkins remained silent for quite a few minutes, contemplating how best to proceed.

"I see your reputation is well founded, Superintendent."

"I don't know anything about that, but I do know that you haven't flown over here in a military aircraft just for a holiday. So, are we going to be straight with each other, or not?"

"OK. As I hinted at previously, Dunne was working for MI5. His task was to infiltrate a gang of diamond smugglers who are dealing in blood diamonds."

"Where were the proceeds going?" Hays asked.

"We believe some of it was going to a small terrorist cell in the Middle East. They have been responsible for some very nasty outrages in a number of European cities. It's what we refer to as a black flag operation, and we'd very much like to cut off their source of funds."

"Hmm... I see. Have you any idea who may have been responsible for Dunne's death?" Hays said.

"How's your investigation going?"

Hays smiled, but said nothing. He reckoned the man couldn't help himself.

"Sorry," Watkins said, "we know that the diamonds are being sourced in Africa. They get smuggled out of there by inserting them into small figurines during manufacture which are described as artists' models. These things don't attract much attention. They generally travel around with the artists as part of their exhibits for various shows, just like out in Clifden. We think some of these stones are finding their way into the retail trade in Ireland and the UK. So, there's an element of money laundering involved too," Watkins said.

"One of my officers has made contact with a Vincent Henderson who seems to be involved in some way, although we don't know if he had anything to do with Dunne's death. At least, we have no strong evidence although there may well be a connection."

"How was Dunne killed?"

"That's where it gets a bit loopy. It seems he was asphyxiated by someone holding a small nitrogen-filled fire extinguisher over his mouth and nose. Very unusual."

"Interesting. I'll ask my people to run that through our database and see if we can come up with any other similar cases," Watkins said.

"That's the trouble. Obviously, there were loads of visitors to the art festival from all over, so it's very difficult to narrow it down. I doubt if it was a local that was responsible."

"What about this Henderson bloke?" Watkins said.

"We're looking into him and his connections at the moment. I should have some more information on him over the next few days. How long are you planning to be in Ireland?"

"As long as it takes, Mr Hays," Watkins said, smiling, "have you any other lines of enquiry?"

"We are following another couple of leads, but I'm not in a position to discuss them just at the moment. What I'd like to know is what MI5 can do to help me to solve a murder. As for the diamond smuggling, I'm inclined to leave that to you for now, unless another crime has been committed on my patch," Hays said.

"I'd like to think that we had your co-operation, Mr Hays. These people need to be stopped, and they obviously have some connection to Galway."

"Maybe, and maybe not. It could just be unfortunate that they decided to take out your man here. Was he doing any good, anyway, before he got killed?" Hays said.

"Oh, yes, he was indeed. He had supplied a good deal of useful information to us. But if you could apprehend his killer, we would be in a much stronger position. We could interrogate the killer to tell us who he was acting for, among other things."

"If we do find whoever killed Dunne – is that his real name by the way?"

"He had a number of different identities."

"Well, if we do find the killer, the Garda Síochána will do their own questioning using traditional methods, and if he's brought to court and convicted, it could be fifteen years before you get your hands on him, or her."

"Hmm... we'll see. But now, Mr Hays, I'm sure you have work to do. I'd appreciate if you would keep me informed of progress, and I will, of course, do the same," Watkins said.

"What are your plans, Mr Watkins?"

"Oh, I'll stay here for a few more days and carry out my own investigations. I won't get in your way, don't worry."

"Very well. I have your phone number from earlier when you called me. I'll be in touch."

Hays got up and bade the man goodbye. They shook hands again, and Hays left.

Chapter Twenty-five

When Hays got back to his office, he picked up his mobile phone which he had left on his desk when he went to meet Watkins at the hotel. There were three missed calls, all from Lyons and a voicemail message that had arrived some ten minutes earlier. He dialled the number in the text message, and listened.

"Mick, it's me. Look there's a really bad situation here. I need you to call me urgently. Where the hell are you anyway?" his partner's voice said.

He hung up and dialled her number.

Lyons explained what had happened with Sinéad Loughran.

"Mick, this is very bad. I need help here, and now would be good," Lyons said.

"OK. I'm on it. I'll call a DI from Pearse Street. He's a mate of mine. Willie McNee by name. Keep your phone free, and I'll have him call you, provided I can get through to him. He's a top man. He'll sort this out, and try not to worry, love."

"OK. Thanks, Mick."

Lyons sat back into her car. She wasn't sure exactly where she was, but she knew she was only about fifteen minutes away from Merrion Square. She was terribly restless, worrying about what fate had befallen her friend and colleague at the hands of Vincent Henderson. She hated not being able to do anything.

Her phone sprang to life. It was a number she didn't recognize.

"Lyons."

"Hi, Maureen. This is Willie McNee from Pearse Street. Mick has been on to me. Sorry to hear about Sinéad, but we'll get it sorted. Do you know what number on Merrion Square Henderson has his office?"

"Hi, Willie, thanks. Yes, I'm fairly sure it's number twenty-two, around the corner from The Merrion Hotel. Are you going there?"

"Yes. I've organized a couple of squad cars and I'll send them up now. Can you find your way back to his office?"

"Yes, don't worry. I'll see you there. And thanks, Willie."

"No problem. I'd better get going."

* * *

When Lyons arrived back at Merrion Square there were two brightly coloured Garda cars stopped in the road outside number twenty-two with their blue lights flashing. Lyons pulled in behind the rearmost one, and set her rather more subtle blue lights going too. She got out and went up the steps to the door and waved her warrant card for the Garda that was posted at the entrance.

There were two rooms leading off the carpeted hallway of the property, and Lyons could hear voices coming from the one towards the back of the building. When she entered the room, she saw a tall, thin man in a grey suit standing over a young woman seated at a desk with the paraphernalia of an office all about her. The man looked up as Lyons approached.

"Hi, Inspector. I'm DI McNee. This very helpful young woman is just about to give me Vincent Henderson's mobile phone number and home address."

He turned back to the woman who scribbled some information down on a spiral notebook and tore out the page, handing it to McNee. He looked at it briefly, and then left the room.

When he was out of earshot, he called a detective of similar rank to himself in Dún Laoghaire Garda Station and passed on the address, requesting immediate attendance at Henderson's house. McNee reckoned that Henderson would in all probability try to flee, but he might need to go home first to collect some belongings and travel documents.

When he returned to the office where Lyons was talking to the young woman, he turned to one of the uniformed officers. "Right. Take the computers and bag them up. And see if there's any correspondence that looks interesting in the other room. I presume that's Mr Henderson's office?"

"Yes," the startled woman said, "but you can't just take all our stuff. We need that for work."

"Listen, love. Your Mr Henderson is a suspect in a murder case. And he's abducted a colleague and done God knows what with her. So, you needn't bother protesting. And while I'm at it, I'm going to get a colleague to interview you too. For all I know, you're up to your neck in this whole mess."

"What mess? What are you talking about? Mr Henderson is a legitimate businessman. This is outrageous!"

As the woman waved her hands about to emphasize her indignation, Lyons noticed rather a large diamond ring on the third finger of her right hand.

"Hmm... I wonder," she said to herself, putting two and two together and getting quite a lot more than four.

* * *

Loughran had never been in a situation anything like this before. Although she had worked on many gruesome and gory murder cases, it was always after the event that she turned up to do her work. This was very different, and she was truly terrified. She calculated from the silence around her, apart from the distant noise of traffic, that her captor had left. But she was securely bound hand and foot, and although she wasn't blindfolded, there was very little light coming into the place where she was being held, so she couldn't see much. The room, if you could call it that, had but one small window beside the door, and that was caked with grime, blocking out most of the natural light.

Straining to see what was around her, she identified the cupboard where Henderson had found the rope and tape to restrain her, but it was at the far side of the room, and she was anything but mobile. With sheer dogged determination, she managed to slide her body across, using her one good leg as a lever on the rough floor, and got herself in a position to use her tethered hands to pull the door of the cupboard open a little. But not being able to see what she was doing with her back to the piece of furniture, and her tied hands with very limited movement, it was hopeless. She sat back against the old wooden press, and tears began to flow down her cheeks. Then she had another idea.

* * *

Vincent Henderson lived on a very upmarket road in Glenageary, on the southside of Dublin, close to Dún Laoghaire, Sandycove and Dalkey. Many of the large, red-brick houses were built in blocks of two, with granite steps up to the front doors, and a generous amount of garden to both the front and rear of the properties. Tall black wrought-iron gates, electrically operated, protected his house from the street; although in fairness, this was a quiet area, with very little crime. When the officers from Dún Laoghaire arrived at the house, they had to use the intercom on the gatepost to gain access to the front of the house. They drove in and stopped. The detective sergeant in charge, who had taken his unambiguous instructions from Willie McNee's associate, trotted up the steps to the front door and rang the bell. His two uniformed colleagues went around the side of the house, to see if there was anyone attempting to depart by the back door.

After a few moments, the door was opened rather gingerly by a short woman dressed in an apron and flat shoes. The woman was clearly not a native. The detective guessed, correctly, that she was most probably from the Philippines.

"We are looking for Mr Henderson. Is he here, please?" the detective said.

"No. He left already. Just now," the woman said. "I have my papers if you want. I get them," she insisted.

"No, no, please, that's not why we are here. Where did Mr Henderson go?"

"I don't know. He in big hurry. Just came in, took stuff and left again. He say nothing."

"Do you know what car he was driving?"

"His car."

"Is there anyone else at home? What about Mrs Henderson?"

"No. She gone too. Two weeks now. She just took off."

"Do you know where she went?"

"No, sorry."

The detective realised that there was little more to be gained from the woman who was obviously a domestic servant of some kind. He thanked her, and asked her if Mr Henderson returned, he should call the Gardaí in Dún Laoghaire at once as they were anxious to speak to him.

Once back in the car, the detective called McNee.

"Hello, sir. I'm at Henderson's house now. I'm afraid we've missed him. There's a housekeeper here but she wasn't much help, I'm afraid. But she did say that he took off in his own car."

"OK. Thanks. We have a stop and detain notice out for him with his car registration anyway, so maybe the roads police will get him. Thanks for trying."

"No problem."

Lyons approached McNee who was now standing on the footpath outside Henderson's office.

"No good news, I presume?" she said.

"No. He's done a bunk. But we might get him yet. He's still driving his own car, so you never know."

"Why do you think he grabbed Sinéad?" Lyons said.

"Probably a distraction. He figured we'd be so busy looking for her that we'd take our eye off him to let him get away. Any news of Loughran anyway?"

"No. Nothing. I've been onto Crumlin Garda and told them what happened. That's the nearest station to where I lost them in the car. God, I feel a right fool, I can tell you," Lyons said.

"Ah, look, don't beat yourself up. What's this Sinéad Loughran like, anyway. Is she resourceful? Tough?"

"Yes and yes. But if this Henderson guy bumped off one of MI5's finest, I doubt if killing Sinéad would cost him a thought."

"I hear you, but don't jump the gun. We don't know if Henderson is the killer yet, and we've no reason to think that he's actually harmed your friend. What do you want to do now? I'm going to take Henderson's stuff back to Pearse Street and start going through it. I might find a clue as to where he's headed."

"OK. I'm going to call Superintendent Hays and have a chat with him. He may have some ideas."

"Right. See you later then."

Chapter Twenty-six

Lyons needed some time to think. She was very worried about Sinéad Loughran, and felt she should be doing something to rescue her. But what? She strolled across the road into the gardens. There were a small number of women dotted around with groups of young children. They were playing amongst the bushes and trees, letting out the occasional shriek as they were discovered in a game of hide and seek. Lyons found a bench and sat down. She thought about Henderson. Where was he likely to flee to? Most likely, he would try to get away via Northern Ireland, she thought. There was virtually no border anymore, so he could drive to Belfast City Airport unhindered, buy a ticket to the UK or Europe and escape easily enough. Alternatively, he could hide out in some remote location close to Dublin and wait till the fuss died down, but she thought that unlikely, as he would have to emerge at some stage, and in any case, he would have had to have set all that up in advance. After a few minutes, she decided to call Mick Hays again.

"Hi, Mick. Any news?"

"Hi, love. No, sorry, but I've put a few things in motion. I've arranged for a helicopter to take to the skies over the area where Sinéad disappeared. They'll use thermal imaging to see if they can locate a heat source anywhere it shouldn't be. And I've informed our colleagues in the North in case Henderson tries to get away through there, and of course, the ferry operators in Dublin too. And I've been onto the Park. They are going to search their CCTV footage for his car, although that's a bit of a long shot. What are you up to?"

Lyons told him about the raid on Henderson's office and the help she was getting from McNee.

"Yes, he's one of the good guys. But let me ask you, do you think Henderson murdered Dunne, or whoever he really is?"

"Jesus, Mick, I don't know. But I do know that we need to find him. He knows where Sinéad is. I'm really worried about her, Mick. I'll never forgive myself if something bad happens," Lyons said, tearing up slightly.

"Try not to worry, love. Sinéad is a very smart woman. Unless she's been badly hurt, she'll be fine," Hays said.

"That's not actually very helpful, Mick. Look, I'll obviously be staying here till this mess is sorted out one way or the other. Have you told Plunkett?"

"I've told him as much as I feel is good for him. He's told me to deal with it."

"Typical. Right, well I best get on. Let me know if you get any more information," Lyons said.

"Yes, of course. Talk later."

* * *

Loughran decided to wait until it was getting dark to put the next stage of her plan into action. She was fairly certain that she was alone at this point, not having heard any movement anywhere on the premises since Henderson had left.

"Cheeky bugger," she said to herself, "he was just going to leave me here to die."

When the light outside began to fade, she used her good leg again to manoeuvre herself over to the door. With her legs for leverage, she managed to work her way into a standing position with her back to the door and the little window. Then, with all her strength, she elbowed the window with a sharp jab, and the glass broke with some of it falling out onto the concrete, leaving a jagged hole in the window frame.

She listened intently for any reaction to the noise, but heard nothing.

Twisting herself into an ungainly stance, she managed to bring her tethered wrists up to the sharp edge of broken glass, and by sawing painfully against the broken window, she eventually managed to free her arms. Her wrists were bleeding quite a bit from her efforts, but she hadn't cut a vein, thank heavens. It was just superficial bleeding from scratches on her skin. She sat down again on the rough floor and used her liberated hands to untie her ankles before ripping the tape from around her mouth in another painful operation. She stretched her limbs to restore her circulation and rubbed her wrists. Then she tried the door which was, of course, locked. She went to the cupboard and rummaged inside and found a short piece of wood. It was like one leg of a wooden chair, or something. Loughran used this to remove the remainder of the glass from the broken window.

She removed her jacket and placed it around the inside of the window frame. Then she climbed up on the sill, and put her legs outside, following through with the rest of her body. At last, she was free, but she had no idea where she was, or if there was anyone watching.

* * *

The helicopter which Hays had arranged was circulating overhead.

"Echo 256. We have an image from a closed yard to the rear of Dolphin's Barn fire station," the pilot said, looking closely at the screen of his thermal imaging set up, where the white shape of a person could clearly be seen.

"Roger Echo 256. Please remain on station. We'll get a car around there as soon as we can."

The helicopter pilot clicked the transmit button on his radio to acknowledge the instruction and brought the machine into a hover 500 feet above the scene.

Loughran heard the throbbing of the helicopter and stood still in the yard, waving her arms to signal that she needed help. It wasn't long before she heard the sound of sirens approaching, and a few seconds later, a squad car pulled up outside the gate.

"Help. Get me out of here. I've been kidnapped!" Loughran shouted, when the car had come to a halt and the officers inside had got out.

Although the gates to the yard that Loughran was standing in were locked, it didn't take the two burly Gardaí long to crash through. Loughran ran into the arms of the first Garda.

"Oh, thank God," she said, before bursting into uncontrollable sobbing.

When she had disentangled herself from the man, she asked if she could use a mobile phone.

"Sit into the car, love. We need to get you to a hospital. You can make the call while we drive down to St Vincent's."

One of the Gardaí stayed behind to secure the yard waiting for the forensic team to arrive and collect whatever evidence may have been left behind from Loughran's forced detention.

When Loughran was seated in the back of the Garda car, she called Lyons on the phone she had been lent.

"Hey, Maureen, it's Sinéad."

"Jesus, Sinéad, where the hell are you?"

"I'm in the back of a Garda car being driven to St Vincent's Hospital for a check-up. But I'm OK, really. Have you tracked down Henderson?"

"Never mind him. What about you? Did he hurt you, Sinéad?"

"No, not really. He tied me up and gagged me, but he wasn't very good at it. I'm fine really. Where are you?"

"I'm at Merrion Square. But I'll come down to the hospital now. I'll be there in a few minutes. What ward are you in?"

"I'll just be in A & E, I imagine. I hope there's a hunky young doctor to look after me!"

"That's my girl. OK, great. See ya."

Lyons was pleased to hear that her colleague's spirit wasn't broken by her ordeal.

Chapter Twenty-seven

Henderson had left Dublin soon after he visited his house in Glenageary. He had swapped his luxurious Jaguar for a small white Peugeot van that he kept fully fuelled in a lock-up a couple of kilometres from his home for just such an occasion. It was noisy, and smelled of diesel oil, but it would do the job all the same. He pulled a dark-coloured baseball cap down low over his forehead, and set off.

He drove to Cork in the south of the country arriving as night was falling. He located a cheap bed and breakfast place out at Ballycureen on the Kinsale Road, and paid in advance, in cash, much to the delight of the rather portly woman who ran the place. He used the name Victor Harrington, and told his host that he would not be needing breakfast, as he was leaving very early in the morning. She was not displeased.

At six in the morning Henderson let himself out of the bungalow quietly and retrieved the van which he had parked around the back of the place out of sight. He drove to Cork Airport which was just a few kilometres further on, and parked in the public car park, leaving the ticket in the van. Once inside, he studied the departures board, and then went to the Aer Lingus desk and purchased a ticket to

London Heathrow for a departure at 8:45. The flight cost him over two hundred euro, which was expensive, but such was the way of things for last-minute sales in this era of so called 'low-cost carriers'.

At ten past eight, when he had eaten a rather mediocre breakfast, saved only by the excellent quality of the accompanying coffee, the flight was called, and Henderson made his way to the departure gate where he boarded the Airbus A320 without incident. The flight was barely one third full, so Henderson took a window seat in row 10, pleased to see that he was alone in a block of three. At 8:35 the steward at the front of the aircraft began closing the forward door and confirming with his colleagues that the rear entrance was closed and the slides were armed. Just before he sealed the aircraft in preparation for departure, another passenger came marching down the jetway and the door was pushed open again to admit the man. The new arrival exchanged a few words with the steward, and then started down the aisle. At row 10 he sat down, and Henderson was puzzled to observe that the man chose the seat next to him, and not the aisle seat, which would have been much more usual in this situation. Henderson turned to his new companion frowning, but the man simply busied himself with fastening his seatbelt and avoided eye contact with Henderson altogether.

The aircraft pushed back at exactly 8:45, and as it taxied towards the departure runway, announcements concerning safety were rattled out over the loudspeakers which were duly ignored by just about everyone on board. The cabin staff drew attention to the safety leaflet in the pockets of the seats, demonstrated how to put on a lifejacket, and patrolled the cabin to ensure that everyone had their belt fastened. Without further ado, the plane accelerated down the runway and became airborne at 8:56, banking to the left as soon as it was clear of the airfield, and headed for London.

Once the flight was established the man sitting beside Henderson reached into his small cabin bag and took out a set of handcuffs. He caught Henderson completely off-guard, and by the time Henderson realised what was happening he was manacled to the arm rest of his seat.

"Who the hell are you, and what do you think you are doing?" Henderson blurted out as his face reddened with anger.

"Good morning, Mr Henderson. My name is Roger Watkins. I work for the British Government. You are under arrest, but I think you may have already figured that out. Now why don't you sit back and enjoy your flight, as they say. It's the most comfortable you are likely to be for the next several days, of that I can assure you."

"You can't do that. I'm an EU citizen. You have no jurisdiction. And anyway, what's the charge?" Henderson said. He was by this time very irate.

"That's the wonderful thing about international flights. It takes the lawyers months to figure out who exactly has jurisdiction, as you call it, especially now that the UK is no longer part of the European Union. By the time they work it all out, it will be too late for you, Mr Henderson. Now be quiet. I want to get some sleep."

The flight proceeded uneventfully, landing at Heathrow at 10:10. The aircraft taxied to the gate, and as it docked, the steward at the front of the cabin made another announcement.

"Ladies and gentlemen, could I ask you to remain seated for a few minutes. We have a procedural issue to deal with before you can disembark. It won't take long, so please remain seated for now till I make a further announcement."

The passengers weren't happy, but did as they were told, muttering unkind words to each other and under their breath. The forward door was opened, and two burly men dressed in black uniforms with black hats bearing the word 'Police' and carrying sub-machine guns entered the cabin. They approached row 10. Watkins handed over the keys to Henderson's handcuffs, got up from his seat and collected his carry-on bag.

"Thanks, lads," he said. "Over to you now."

When Watkins had left the plane, Henderson was manhandled off too, and was taken down a set of steps connected to the jetway, bundled into an unmarked black van, and driven away.

He might have expected to be taken to a police station close to Heathrow. Hounslow, perhaps, or maybe Uxbridge, or even the police station within the footprint of the airport, but that's not what happened. Instead, he was driven to an old, and apparently abandoned facility on the appropriately named Dick Turpin Way at Feltham, adjacent to the airport. The van drove through a set of high wooden gates into a yard where there was an old barn and a series of what looked like stables. He was taken from the van and brought into one of these buildings. But once inside, he observed that the place was anything but a disused farm. In contrast to the shabby exterior, the inside of the premises was modern, well populated, sparklingly clean, and bristling with all kinds of technology. It was brightly lit, and several people appeared to be busy at PCs and telephones. The two policemen that had removed Henderson from the Aer Lingus flight marched him to what looked like a reception desk. A woman in her late forties or early fifties sat behind an oak table, surrounded by PC screens and TV monitors.

"This is Mr Victor Henderson, Irene. He'll be staying here with us for a few days to help us with our enquiries. Be gentle with him!" the man said with a grin.

"Where am I? You can't just kidnap me like this. It's completely illegal. I want a lawyer."

"I see, sir," Irene said. "So, it was OK for you to take a forensic officer – Ms Loughran by name – tie her up and dump her in an appallingly dirty outhouse without food or water, but it's not OK for us to bring you here to what, as you will see, is more like a four-star hotel?"

Henderson just grunted, but he wondered how they knew so much about him. What else did they know, and who exactly were his captors?

* * *

When Henderson had been photographed and fingerprinted, and a DNA swab taken from his mouth, he was accompanied to a windowless room by a man who carried with him some men's clothing, wrapped in clear plastic.

"You need to remove your clothes. Everything, shoes and all. Put these on," he said, proffering the plastic bag to Henderson.

"Not my shoes. I need orthopaedic footwear. I have a slightly deformed left foot," Henderson said.

"Everything, Mr Henderson. And that includes both shoes. It's not up for debate."

Henderson detected a coldness in the man's demeanour, so he very reluctantly complied.

* * *

In Feltham, Henderson's clothes had been given to the forensic team and were being closely examined, with photographs and full details of each item being carefully recorded.

"Did this guy say he had a problem with his feet?" Terry Barker, the forensic technician said to his assistant, Amy Langwood.

"Yeah. Something about his left foot being a bit skewy, I think."

Barker examined the left shoe carefully. He pulled up the insole that was sitting snugly inside, and examined underneath.

"Hang on. Amy, there's something here," he exclaimed to Langwood who was suddenly taking more of an interest. "Give me that Stanley knife here, a sec."

Amy Langwood handed him the implement, making sure that the blade was retracted. Terry Barker used the knife to cut around the shape of the heel, and lifted out a piece of leather. He then used his index finger to prise out a small plastic bag which he put beside the shoe on his bench. He carefully opened the bag, and tipped out the contents. A dozen sparkling diamonds spilled out onto the bench and rolled around.

"Wow! Nice one, Terry. I wonder if there are any more in the other shoe?"

Barker examined the second shoe carefully, but there were no more treasures to be found.

Chapter Twenty-eight

After Loughran had received a triage examination from a nurse in St Vincent's emergency department, it was decided that her wounds just needed to be cleaned out and dressed, and her ankle strapped up. There appeared to be no lasting damage, Loughran was advised to keep her forearms dry when showering, and waterproof, elasticated plastic covers were supplied to ensure that her bandages didn't get wet.

Lyons arrived just as the bandages were being applied in a cubicle within the emergency department.

"Look at you," Lyons said when she saw her colleague. "Boy, am I glad to see you." She lent in awkwardly past the nurse and gave Loughran a hug.

"Any sign of yer man?" Loughran said.

"Nope! Not a vestige. He's either done a bunk, or he's holed up in some hideaway somewhere. But don't worry, we'll get him yet."

Lyons turned to the nurse who was making a particularly neat job of bandaging up Loughran's wounded arms.

"Will you be keeping Ms Loughran in, nurse?"

"No, that won't be necessary. But has she somewhere to go where she can give these a chance to heal for a few days?"

"Yes, of course. That won't be a problem. You're coming home with me, girl," Lyons said.

"Just to warn you, Maureen, I'm a lousy patient. I'll drive you mad."

"Probably. But if you don't behave, I'll set Mick on you. He'll soon sort you out."

Loughran smiled at her friend. She knew Mick would be just as supportive and would do anything he could to speed her recovery.

Forty minutes later, after the nurse had finished with her, and they had signed a waiver of liability on discharge, the two women left the hospital and made for Lyons' car which was parked in the multi-storey car park across from the main entrance. Loughran was limping a bit, but she still managed to make reasonable progress.

"It's pretty late, Sinéad. Do you want to find a hotel for the night? Somewhere nice. My treat," Lyons said as they sat into her Volvo.

"Listen, I know this is mean, Maureen, but any chance we could get back to Galway? I've had enough of the big city bright lights, to do me for a good few years."

"Yes, sure. I'll call Mick once we're on the road, and get him to turn on your electric blanket."

As they set off, Lyons wanted to find out a bit more about her colleague's abduction.

"Did Henderson say anything to you when you got into the car at first? Before he started roughing you up, I mean."

"Not much, to be honest. But he did say something that I thought was a bit odd," Loughran said.

"What was that?"

"He said something like 'I didn't have anything to do with the murder of Adam Dunne. When this is all over, you'll find out who is on whose side, just wait till you see.' Then he went quiet."

"Hmm... that's a bit odd, but he's obviously up to his neck in the diamond thing. Don't forget we saw him out at the coastguard station."

"Yes, I know. But that's why I don't understand what he meant."

The two women returned to their own thoughts as they drove along the M6 towards Galway.

The traffic was light travelling from east to west that night. Even when they got to the outskirts of Galway, there wasn't much around, though by this time it was the small hours, so it was no great surprise. Lyons drove to her house in Salthill. Hays had stayed up to welcome the two women, and made a fuss of Loughran, offering to brew coffee or even cook her a meal if that was what she needed.

"No, thanks, Mick. I'll just get a glass of water and take a couple of paracetamol. I'm all in, to be honest. And thanks, both of you."

They all agreed to park the case for the night and go off to bed. Tomorrow, they would convene at Mill Street and have a thorough evaluation of events.

Chapter Twenty-nine

The following morning, Hays, Lyons and Loughran drove from Salthill to the Garda station at Mill Street in the centre of Galway.

"Thanks very much for letting me stay, folks," Loughran said as Hays parked his car. "I think I'll go across to the lab and catch up on whatever has been going on there. I'll see you later, OK?"

"Yes, Sinéad, of course. But take it easy today, won't you. Give your wounds a chance to heal properly," Lyons said.

"I'll be fine, thanks."

Hays and Lyons went inside to Lyons' office.

"Do you mind if I stay for a few minutes? I'd like to see what the team has been up to while you were otherwise occupied," Hays said.

"No, of course not. I'd be very glad of your input," Lyons replied.

Their relationship was odd, in that when they were working, they assumed the roles of superintendent and senior inspector, and behaved as if they were just colleagues. But as soon as they left work, they behaved like man and wife, with a little bit of teenage nonsense thrown in for good measure. The arrangement worked really well, although if you had asked either of them, they would not have been able to account for it.

Lyons gathered her team around her in the open plan while Hays literally took a back seat.

"OK, everyone. I need an update from you on this whole mess, and let's start with you, Sally."

"OK, boss. But can I ask how Sinéad is? We heard she got into real trouble over in Dublin."

"She's OK thanks, Sally. Yes, it was a bit rough there for a while, but she'll be fine. Now, let's get on. What have you got for us?"

"Not much really. Sorry, but the whole thing seems to be a dead end," Fahy said, a little embarrassed that she had nothing more positive to report.

"Did we get anything from Dunne's phone?"

"Not really. Just a few local numbers in Clifden in the call history, oh, and two calls to a UK number, but it must have been a burner, because it's unobtainable now. But it was pretty clean. I'd say he wiped it regularly."

"OK. Well, for today, I want you to concentrate on Vincent Henderson. I want to know all about him. Bank accounts; company accounts; phone records; his travel for the past year; his relationships, both personal and other; and anything else you can dig up on him. The Dublin lads collected a pile of stuff from his office, so give Inspector McNee a call in Pearse Street and see if there was anything interesting in that lot."

"Right, boss, I'll get to it as soon as we're finished here."

"Eamon – anything?" Lyons said.

"Maybe. Keith from forensics called me yesterday morning. He had a bit more information about the fire extinguisher, so I managed to track down a distributor in the UK that apparently supply a couple of places in Ireland."

"Nice work. Anything of interest?" Lyons said.

"Well, there are only two stockists of that particular item that the distributor is aware of, though they did say that some other outlets could have brought it indirectly themselves, but they thought that unlikely. It's not a big seller."

"And where are these two outlets as you call them?" Lyons said, wishing Flynn would get on with it.

"One is in Tipperary. It's some kind of farm co-operative near Thurles, but the other is a bit more interesting. It's Blue Dolphin Marine here in Galway. They have a chandlery down near the docks on St Nicholas Street. It's quite a big outfit from what I can gather."

Lyons turned to look at her partner.

"Yes, I know them. I get some stuff there for my boat from time to time. It's run by a man called Ron O'Sullivan. He's a decent sort from what I know of him," Hays said.

"Would you like to pay him a visit, sir?" Lyons said.

"Perhaps it would be better if Eamon made the call. I don't really want to mix business and leisure, if you see what I mean. But if you need any sort of follow up, let me know, and I'll get stuck in."

"Right, Eamon. That's your mission for the day. Find out if Blue Dolphin Marine sold any of those extinguishers recently, and if so, to whom," Lyons said.

"Superintendent, have you heard anything more from the English guy who was snooping around?" Lyons asked.

"No, I haven't. I tried to call him yesterday on the number he gave me, but it seems that phone was defunct. It may have been a burner that he did away with. I'll try again later to see if I can establish contact."

"So, has anyone got any sign of Vincent Henderson anywhere? We need to find him, and soon. Any news from the Northern Ireland police, the airlines or the ferry operators?"

"No, nothing, boss. But I'll call the PSNI again shortly in case they have anything. If he's left the country, that would be the most obvious route," Flynn said.

"Yes, do please, Eamon, and let me know immediately if we get anything. OK, everyone, that's it for now. You know what you have to do. Let's meet up again at five o'clock and discuss progress. Thanks," Lyons said.

Hays excused himself and went up to his own office on the third floor, and Lyons went to hers.

* * *

It was late morning when Hays' mobile phone rang. He looked at the screen before answering, but the number was withheld. He pressed the little green receiver icon on the phone.

"Hello."

"Ah, good morning, Superintendent. This is Watkins here. I thought I'd just give you a call with some news."

"Good morning, Mr Watkins. What is there to report?"

"I'm sure you'll be pleased to hear that we arrested Vincent Henderson this morning at Heathrow. He was on an inbound flight from Cork."

"Cork! Wow, we didn't see that coming. We usually see absconders departing via Northern Ireland. Can we come and get him?" Hays said.

"Eh, not for the moment. We need to have a candid chat with him about all this smuggling. I should mention that he had over a hundred thousand pounds' worth of diamonds hidden in one of his shoes."

"I see. But he may have murdered one of your associates here in Ireland. We need to get him back here to question him properly, Mr Watkins."

"All in good time, Superintendent. I'll let you know when we have finished with him."

"Can you at least tell me what police station he is being held at?"

"He's in a nice, discreet, and very secure facility in England, Superintendent. Don't worry, he won't be going anywhere. Now I really must dash. Bye."

The line went dead.

Chapter Thirty

Blue Dolphin Marine occupied a spacious premises on the narrow street leading to the waterfront in Galway's docklands. It was a double-fronted shop with all kinds of marine equipment on display. Despite the narrowness of the footpath outside the shop, the owner had managed to bring some of his wares outside in an effort to tempt passing pedestrians to come in and hopefully buy something. But the sailing fraternity of Galway kept the business ticking over, and O'Sullivan had negotiated good contracts with a few shipping companies that used the harbour, which paid handsomely for his services.

Eamon Flynn entered the shop and started to browse. As he scanned the shelves, he observed a man in his fifties with a round, ruddy face and a smattering of grey hair, dressed in a check shirt and blue jeans behind the counter. As Flynn made his way up along the rather cramped aisle, the man smiled at him.

"Morning. Can I help you at all?"

"I'll be with you in a minute," Flynn said. He continued to scan the extensive stock packed into the place, and then, as he approached the counter, there on a shelf he saw three of the items he was looking for. He picked up one of the red and yellow cans, with 'Flameout' written in large letters across it against a background of flames painted on the outside. The tin had a conical-shaped black rubber attachment where the contents of the extinguisher would emerge, and a yellow plastic seal around the press-button. Flynn took the item to the counter.

"A very handy piece of kit," O'Sullivan said, "I wish more people would have one of those things handy on board. A fire at sea is a terrible thing."

"Do you not sell many of them then?" Flynn said.

"No, we don't. A good few sailors have bigger extinguishers, but that one is very easy to use, and it doesn't leave powder all over the place. It's pure nitrogen. And most boat fires start small in any case. Usually at the cooker or the fuel lines, and there's always someone close by. That little can has about a minute's worth of stuff in it, and that would take care of most small fires very quickly."

Flynn thought that now would be a good time to introduce himself to the proprietor. He held up his warrant card.

"I'm Detective Inspector Flynn, Mr O'Sullivan. May I ask how many of these you have sold in the last month or so?"

"Oh, right, Inspector. Well, I don't remember to be honest. I can't keep track of everything that we sell here. But our stock control system should tell us. Hang on a minute."

O'Sullivan went behind a partially glazed wall into an office of sorts and started fiddling with a desktop computer. A moment later he was back.

"We sold one about three weeks ago. That leaves three on the shelf, and when we sell another one, I'll have to reorder them. But I doubt if they'll be flying out coming into winter."

"And was that on an account, or a debit card?"

"Hang on, I'll have a look again."

O'Sullivan went back into the office and re-examined his machine.

"'twas a cash sale. What's your interest anyway, Inspector?"

"How much do these cost?" Flynn said, dodging the question.

"Yours for a mere 29.99. Not much when you think it could save your vessel and maybe your life, eh?"

"Very well. I'll take this one so," Flynn said reaching into his pocket for his debit card. O'Sullivan rang the purchase up on the till and Flynn tapped his card on the machine to complete the purchase.

"Will you be wanting a receipt?" O'Sullivan said.

"Yes please. And by the way, do you have CCTV here at all?"

O'Sullivan tore off a small, printed receipt and handed it to Flynn.

"We do. Mind you it's not a whole lot of use. More a deterrent than anything else. If the buggers want to rob you then that's what they'll do."

"Would you have the CCTV footage from the day that this thing was sold last?"

"Yes, I can get it for you. It will take a few minutes if you don't mind waiting. I'll get Aoibhín to copy it onto a DVD for you. I'm not great with technology, unless it's seafaring gear."

O'Sullivan went back into the office and summoned Aoibhín who was further out the back of the shop unpacking stock. She came into the office and went to the PC.

Back at the counter, O'Sullivan continued to chat.

"Do you work with Michael Hays at all, Inspector?"

"Yes. He's my boss two levels up. Do you know him?"

"I do, to be sure. Isn't he always in here during the summer getting bits and bobs for his boat. And I serviced his engine at the start of the summer too. It's a fine yacht he has there. I heard tell that his girlfriend bought it for him out of some prize she won for bravery or something. She must be a right character."

Flynn didn't want to get into a discussion about Senior Inspector Maureen Lyons with the man, so he deftly changed the subject.

"I suppose you'll be slack enough for the next few months then?" he said.

"Ah, not really. We have a stock take to do in another week or so. And then all the new stuff for next season will be arriving, and that will all have to be checked and unpacked. And you'd be surprised how the place keeps ticking over, even in the winter. The sailing club has a brass monkey series starting at the end of September, and we always sell a good bit of warm gear coming up to that. And if the weather is blowy, fellas will break their rigging too and it will need replacing. It keeps us going."

Aoibhín eventually emerged from the office and gave Flynn a shiny DVD wrapped in a see-through sleeve.

"It should play with VLC on any computer, but if you can't get it to work, come back and I'll convert it to another format," the girl said rather shyly.

"Thanks very much."

Flynn turned to leave, and O'Sullivan called to him as he was making his way back towards the door, "Give my best regards to Mick, now, won't you?"

Flynn just waved.

Chapter Thirty-one

"Hello, Séan. It's me."

Mulholland recognised Lyons' voice immediately.

"Ah, hello, Maureen. I hear you had some sport over in Dublin. Is Sinéad OK?"

"Yes, she's fine, but it wasn't nice. Listen, Séan, I need you to do something for me. Can you find out where the town council take the rubbish from the showgrounds during the festival. I spotted a good few bins dotted around the place, and I presume they empty them either during or at the end of the event."

"God, Maureen, I'm sure they do. Let me make some enquiries. What is it you're after anyway?"

"I'm going to send you a photograph of a small portable fire extinguisher. We think that it was the murder weapon used to kill Adam Dunne. I want to see if someone can find it amongst the rubbish if it hasn't been disposed of yet. We might just get lucky."

"And by 'someone', I'm guessing you mean me?" Mulholland said.

"Yes, or one of your men, Séan. I wouldn't ask, but it's important."

"Right, so. I'll get Peadar onto it straight away."

"Thanks, Séan. Oh, and by the way, did forensics find anything out at the coastguard station?"

"They found a couple of figurines that were partly destroyed. The had been sawn open, and there was evidence that something might have been hidden in them, but there was no sign of whatever it was."

"Did they collect fingerprints, or anything?" Lyons said.

"I think so. You should check with the forensic lab in Galway. They'll have the details."

"OK, thanks. I'll just go and take a picture of the fire extinguisher and get it off to you."

"Righto. I'll talk to you later, Maureen."

"Bye, Séan."

Lyons went out to the open plan where Eamon Flynn was sitting at his desk studying a video on his office PC. The Flameout cannister that he had purchased was sitting beside his computer on the desk. Lyons took a shot of the red and yellow cylinder with her phone and sent the picture on to Séan Mulholland.

"What are you looking at there, Eamon?"

"It's the CCTV I brought back from the chandlery place down on St Nicholas Street. It was recorded the day that this thing was sold," Flynn said pointing to the Flameout tin on the desk.

"We don't have a recording of the actual purchase. The camera is aimed at the body of the shop, not the till. But I thought we might get something from the comings and goings on the day."

"OK, well, keep looking."

Lyons was about to leave, when she saw something on the screen that she recognised.

"Hang on, Eamon. Wind it back a bit. Yes, that's it. Hold it there."

Flynn paused the video.

"Unless I'm much mistaken, that is the guy from the Clifden Arts Festival, what's his name, Arbuthnot. That's it, Mathew Arbuthnot."

"Are you sure?" Flynn said.

"Yes. Well at least I think so. Can you enhance it at all?"

"I can't, but I know a man who can. Let me give it to John O'Connor. He's great with these things. Leave it with me for half an hour."

"Thanks, Eamon. Let me know when you have a clearer picture."

* * *

Garda Peadar Tobin had been given the task of trying to find the discarded murder weapon amongst the thrash that had been collected from the showgrounds on the days following the murder.

He started by calling to the Clifden Area Offices of Galway County Council located on Market Street. The administrators at the office told him to go around to the rear of the building where there was a spacious yard with several vehicles parked, and look for a Liam Nevins, who was in charge of the team that collected refuse in the town. Nevins was having a cup of tea with a few colleagues. He was dressed in an orange high-vis jacket and indescribably dirty jeans, with muddy boots on his feet.

"Liam Nevins," Tobin called out to the group.

"That's me! Who's asking?"

"Garda Peadar Tobin, Mr Nevins. Can you spare me a moment?"

"Of course, Guard. Would you like a mug of tea?" Nevins asked.

"No, you're grand. I need to know about the rubbish that was collected from the showgrounds during the festival. Can you tell me what happened to it?"

"We have one of those huge trailers down by the harbour. We collect the bags from all around, and bring them down to the trailer. Then, when the thing is full, we call the waste disposal company and they come and lift it and take it off to their depot for recycling and incineration."

"How often is it taken away, this big trailer thing?" Tobin said.

"It depends on how much crap we've collected, doesn't it. But usually about once every three weeks. More often in the high summer though. But we got an empty one in just before the festival, so I imagine it's less than half full just now. Have you lost something Guard?" Nevins said. He looked around, grinning, at his companions for their approval at his scintillating wit.

"Tell ye what lads. I need a hand to try and find a particular item that may be in that lot down in the trailer. There's a drink in it for anyone who wants to lend me a hand."

There were a few moments silence as the group contemplated the offer.

"Fair enough. C'mon, men. We'll give the man a hand to find whatever it is. As it happens, you might be in luck," Nevins said.

"How's that?"

"The plastic bags we use for the litter bins in the town are white with the council logo printed on them. But the ones we used for the festival were black, because the bins were bigger, and the white bags don't fit."

"OK. Well, can we go then?" Tobin said.

* * *

It was mid-afternoon when Eamon Flynn stuck his head around the door of Lyons' office.

"Got a minute, boss?" he said.

"Yes, sure, come in. What's up?"

Flynn handed Lyons a piece of paper on which there was a photograph of a man. He was tall, and very upright, and he was wearing an overcoat.

"That's yer man from the CCTV at Blue Dolphin. Do you recognise him?"

"I do indeed. It's definitely Arbuthnot. Well done, Eamon."

"Don't thank me, boss, it was all O'Connor's work to be honest. What do you reckon?"

"I think we need a wee chat with Mathew Arbuthnot, don't you? But let's wait till we see if Séan has any luck finding the fire extinguisher out beyond," Lyons said.

"Right. Let me know what you want me to do," Flynn said, and left the room.

Chapter Thirty-two

Mick Hays wasn't happy. He went in search of his boss, Superintendent Finbarr Plunkett, and found him in his office.

"Come in, Mick. Take a seat. What's on your mind?"

"Thanks, sir. Can I talk to you about this Vincent Henderson character?"

"Henderson. He's the suspect for the murder out in Clifden, is that right?" Plunkett said.

"Yes, that's him. There's something going on with diamond smuggling that he seems to have been involved in. But he abducted Sinéad Loughran from outside his offices in Dublin, and kept her locked up in some dingy yard near the canal. Now he's disappeared. There was a man from MI5 in England here, and somehow, he's managed to spirit Henderson away with him. I'm not happy about any of it, sir."

"Hmm... I can see why, too. What was yer man's name from MI5?"

"He called himself Roger Watkins."

Plunkett wrote the name down on his jotter.

"Have you any contacts over there we could talk to, sir? I'd like to get Henderson back. We have some pretty serious charges to lay at his door, and I don't like being made a fool of by that lot."

"I know exactly what you mean, Mick. Neither do I. But MI5 are a bit of a law unto themselves. None of my contacts in the Met would be able to help. But listen. Leave it with me for the rest of the day, and I'll see if there's anything I can do. I might have a word with someone in the department. Is that OK, Mick?"

"Yes, thank you, sir. Anything at all you could do would be appreciated."

Hays got up and left the room, recognising that the meeting was over. But he knew Plunkett well, and he had every faith that the senior man would be able to help in some way.

* * *

"Lyons," she said as she lifted the phone.

"Hello, Maureen. It's Séan here. I have some good news for you. Peadar Tobin went in search of the used fire extinguisher you were after and he had some luck. Apparently, the refuse from the festival was carried off to some big container somewhere and it hadn't been taken away. Tobin got a couple of lads from the council to go through the bags, and they found the little fire extinguisher just as you said. What do you want me to do with it?"

"That's great, Séan. Thank Peadar for me. But listen, we need to get it into the hands of our forensic team as soon as possible. Any chance you could get Peadar to bag it up and drop it off with Sinéad?"

"Yes, I suppose so. I could get it in this afternoon. Would that be OK?"

"Perfect. Thanks a million."

"You're welcome."

When she had finished speaking to Mulholland, she called Loughran and told her to expect the consignment.

"When it arrives, give it a good going over for prints and DNA. The victim may have spat into the rubber bit as he was choking."

"OK. I'll make sure it's done properly," Loughran said.

"Have we any of Henderson's prints on file, Sinéad?"

"I don't think so. But I could get onto Dublin. I'm sure they will have them from his office," Loughran said.

"Good idea. And ask them if they've found his Jaguar while you're on to them, too. If you speak to Inspector McNee, he'll sort it out for you."

"OK. Great. Talk later."

As Lyons finished the call, Superintendent Hays appeared at her door.

"Got a minute?" he said.

"Sure, come in. Grab a seat. What's up?"

Hays relayed the conversations he had had with Watkins and Finbarr Plunkett.

"Bloody hell, Mick. Can we get the bugger back?"

"I'm not sure. Plunkett is going to see if he can pull some strings, but I'm not entirely hopeful. It won't be long before this becomes some sort of political football between us and the Brits, and as you know, that could go either way. But he will do his best for us. He doesn't like it either."

"Did he say as much?"

"No, but I could tell by the look on his face."

"OK, well I guess we'll just have to wait and see."

"Any other developments?" Hays said.

"Well, we got what we believe may be the murder weapon out in a rubbish skip in Clifden. And there's just a slight chance that Mathew Arbuthnot is somehow involved, but I'm not sure."

"Christ, go easy on that one, Maureen. Yer man has some pretty impressive connections. Let me know if you're planning to make a move on him. It could be very tricky."

"I hear you. But if there's any evidence, apart from the fact that he was in the shop where the fire extinguisher was purchased at around the same time, I'll be talking to him, connections or not."

"God help the poor fellow! He's in for the 'Maureen Lyons' treatment," Hays said, smiling. "But let me know first, won't you?"

"Yes, OK. Now I'd better go and see what McNee recovered from Henderson's house and office. Is that everything?"

"Yes, for now. Catch you later."

Chapter Thirty-three

Lyons went out to the open plan where Sally Fahy was seated at her desk.

"Hi, Sally. Cheer me up. Tell me what you've found out about our Mr Henderson."

"Hi, boss. Quite a lot, and not much, really," Fahy said.

Lyons looked puzzled.

"Explain."

"Well, first off, that office he keeps in Merrion Square is some kind of a front. Inspector McNee told me they recovered almost nothing from it. A few petrol receipts, and a couple of letters to the landlord, and that's about it. Same for his PC. Nada."

"And the good news?" Lyons said.

"There isn't any, I'm afraid. We checked out the Jaguar. It's down as being written off two years ago. Scrapped."

"But I'm sure I saw an up-to-date tax disc in the windscreen when it was parked outside his office."

"Probably. You can buy those on the internet for a tenner these days, and it's just as well, because the road tax on that beast is nearly two thousand euro," Fahy said.

"I'm not even going to ask how you know that, Sally. What about his house?"

"More or less the same story. It's rented. He took a six-month lease on the place eight months ago. It's been on month-to-month since then. But there was nothing at all useful in the place. A few bits and bobs, but nothing that's any good to us."

"Who is the landlord of the house?"

"Some outfit called Sylvan Propriété. It's a French name, but they're registered in Jersey, so no information available without a court order, and we won't get that. They like their privacy, that lot."

"Anything from his phone provider, bank, or utility companies, Sally? Give me something."

"Sorry, boss."

"For heaven's sake, Sally. This thing just gets weirder and weirder."

Lyons went back to her office. As was her practice when things weren't making sense, she retrieved the sheet of paper and updated her spider diagram. Adam Dunne was still in the middle, but she added new lines left and right to diamonds; Vincent Henderson; Roger Watkins; and, in a smaller oval on the page, Mathew Arbuthnot; the Clifden Arts Festival; and she even added Charlie Gifford, the groundsman, in for good measure. She was doodling away finding it hard to make any sense of it when Loughran popped her head around the door.

"Busy?" Sinéad said. Despite her recent ordeal, it was clear that her bubbly personality had not been suppressed. She was bright and cheerful as usual.

"Hi, Sinéad. No, not really, just a bit fed up. Come in. How's your arm?"

"Ah, it's fine. I'm just keeping the bandage on for sympathy," she said, with a twinkle in her eyes.

"Round here? You must be joking. Don't you know that Mick has a rule that no one gets any sympathy unless they have lost at least one limb in the line of duty?"

The two of them laughed for a moment.

"Anyway, what can I do for you? Or more likely, what can you do for me?"

"Do you want the good news or the bad news, Maureen?"

"Never mind all that. Just hit me with what you've got."

"OK. Well, the good news is that the canister that Peadar brought in from Clifden is almost certainly the murder weapon. The little plastic ring we recovered out there fits it to perfection, and it's been fully discharged. And there's more."

"Go on."

"We were able to recover quite good finger and thumbprints from the sides of the can."

"And…?"

"That's the end of the good news. They don't belong to Henderson. I got McNee to send me his dabs by email, and there's no doubt. No match. Sorry!"

"God dammit! Where does that leave us?" Lyons said.

"Would up the proverbial without a whatsit cover it?" Loughran said.

"I'm fed up with this whole thing. Fancy a drive out west?"

"Eh... perhaps not, Maureen, no offence. If you recall the last time we went for a drive I ended up bound and gagged in a dirty outhouse. I think I'll pass, if you don't mind."

"Point taken."

"What are you going to do, anyway?"

"I'm going to take my frustration out on someone who is probably totally innocent and get myself into trouble. How does that sound?" Lyons said.

"Very Maureen!"

And they laughed again.

* * *

On the way out to Clifden in her car, Maureen Lyons called Séan Mulholland.

"Hi, Séan. I'm on my way out to you. I have a delicate little operation that I may need you to help with. Will you be there for an hour or so?"

"Yes, of course, Maureen. What's on?"

"I'll tell you when I get there, Séan. See you shortly," Lyons said, and ended the call.

The drive out to Clifden was splendid as usual. Once Lyons got up onto the heathland west of Oughterard, it was clear that autumn now had a good grip on the land. The heather was in full bloom, and the sheep that grazed along the sides of the road were finding it harder to get any sustenance, as the grass verges had all but stopped growing. But the scenery still held a raw beauty that Lyons loved. The combination of the blue mountains in the distance, the brown gashes in the heathland where turf had been cut over the summer months and left to dry in small heaps at the side of the road, and the many lakes, now shimmering in the autumn breeze, revitalized Lyons like nothing else. By the time she pulled in at the kerb outside Clifden Garda station, she was in much better form.

"Ah, there you are, Maureen," Mulholland said as she entered the building. "Can I get you a cup of tea after your drive?"

"Thanks, Séan, that would be very welcome. God, it's beautiful out here. You live in a fabulous place."

"I know. We're blessed. But don't tell anyone!" he said, smiling.

They sat and chatted about nothing in particular as Mulholland produced two mugs of strong tea, accompanied, as always, by a generous plate of chocolate Goldgrain biscuits.

"So, what's the craic?" he asked eventually.

Lyons lent forward in a conspiratorial manner.

"I need to get Mathew Arbuthnot's fingerprints, Séan."

"Cripes, girl, you like living dangerously. He'll go mad."

"Not if we do it right. The man quite probably has a healthy respect for authority. I'd like one of your lads to go and see him. Tell him we're getting nowhere with the enquiry into Dunne's death, and an edict has been issued from on high that everyone connected to the case has to be fingerprinted for the purposes of elimination. My guess is that he'll go along with it, but if he squeals, tell him to call Superintendent Hays for confirmation. What do you think?"

Mulholland took another mouthful of tea and a bite from a biscuit before replying.

"It might work. Have you lined up Mick?"

"I'll do that now. Do you think you could brief Jim Dolan to do the job?"

"You wouldn't be inclined to go yourself?" Mulholland said, hopefully.

"No. He hates me. We had a bit of a bust up the day we found the body, and I get the impression that he doesn't like women."

Mulholland was about to say 'you can see why', but thought better of it.

"I suppose. When do you want to do this?"

"Now would be good," Lyons said.

Mulholland shifted uneasily in his chair.

"I'll go out and call Mick and tell him to expect a call, if you have a word with Jim."

He finished his tea, stood up and put on his peaked cap, which everyone knew was a sign that the next encounter Mulholland had with anyone was going to be official.

Chapter Thirty-four

Vincent Henderson was brought from the place where he had spent a comfortable morning to an interview room that afternoon. The room was warm, but not oppressively so, carpeted, and had a table with four chairs around it, a skylight in the ceiling, and was subtly lit with LED fittings. Watkins had decided to sit in, even though a man known simply as 'J' would actually be doing the questioning. The interview was not being recorded, though J had a notepad and pen to note any observations as required.

Henderson was invited into the room and offered tea or coffee, which he declined.

J opened the proceedings.

"I trust you are well rested, Mr Henderson?" he said.

Henderson grunted, but said nothing as he took a seat opposite J.

"I think you know Mr Watkins. He'll be present for our chat as an observer. Feel free to ask anything that occurs to you as we proceed. Now, let's get started. Can you explain to me how you've come to have almost a hundred thousand pounds' worth of diamonds about your person?"

"Give me some paper and a loan of you pen, please," Henderson said.

J complied. He tore a clean sheet from his pad, and handed it to Henderson along with the biro.

Henderson scribbled something on the page and handed both back to his interrogator.

"Call this number," he said.

J looked at the page. There was a long series of numbers written on it, which J recognised as a UK mobile number.

"Who's this?" J said.

"Just fucking call it," Henderson replied.

J looked sternly at Henderson. But after a moment, he stood up and left the room. Neither Watkins nor Henderson spoke. A few minutes later, the door opened, and J signalled Watkins to come outside. They stood outside in the corridor with the door to the interview room closed. The door was soundproofed in any case.

"Your man," J said, nodding to the door, "is only one of ours. MI6 of course. The bastards never tell us anything."

"Christ! That's just bloody wonderful. Why didn't he say something to me?"

"That's just the way they behave. The woman I phoned wasn't best pleased. But I told her it was their fault for not keeping us informed."

"What happens to him now?"

"MI6 are going to come and collect him. She said his cover is now blown, so they'll move him to some other region and give him another identity. He's apparently one of their best operatives."

"Do you think he killed Dunne?" Watkins said.

"No, definitely not. Remember, he was one of ours too."

"Is there anyone involved in this mess that isn't one of ours?" Watkins said.

"Yes, there definitely is. But that's not our concern. It seems MI6 have the whole thing ready to pop."

"OK. Good for them. I suppose I'd better let the Paddies know that they've been chasing down the wrong man. Typical."

"Don't tell them too much. Just the basics. We don't want any more trouble than we're already in."

"OK. Bloody hell. What a fiasco," Watkins said as he wandered off, not quite believing what had just happened.

Watkins left it several hours before making the phone call to Mick Hays. He needed to figure out what to say that would explain things, without giving too much away. He knew Hays was smart, and would probably be able to figure things out for himself in any case. It was late afternoon by the time he got to make the call.

"Is that Superintendent Hays?"

Hays had broken off from a tedious task with a spreadsheet to take the call and his mind was still occupied with columns and rows of figures.

"Yes. Who's this please?"

"Watkins."

"Ah, hello, Mr Watkins. What news?"

"I just thought I should let you know that Henderson isn't your man. That is, he had nothing to do with the murder of Adam Dunne."

"I see. And you know this because?"

"Let's just say certain facts have come to light that make it impossible for Henderson to have done it. I can't go into details, but I know this to be the case."

"What's happening to the man, Mr Watkins?"

"You don't need to worry about that, Superintendent. We're looking after him well."

Hays thought for a moment.

"Mr Watkins, I have to say that if our evidence contradicts what you have just told me, I will need to get back in touch with you and possibly escalate the matter further. And Henderson still has some fairly serious charges to face here in Ireland. He did abduct one of our people after all, and treated her very badly."

"Yes. He very much regrets that, and wishes to apologise. But as far as escalation is concerned, that will need to be handled at another level altogether, perhaps via the department, as you call it. As far as we are concerned here, the matter is over," Watkins said.

"Can you at least share whatever you have found from speaking to Henderson? It may be helpful to us with the investigation."

"I'm sorry, Mr Hays, that's not how we operate."

"Can you please give me a number that I can contact you on should we need to?" Hays asked, but the line had gone dead.

Hays slammed the telephone receiver down hard. He saved and closed the spreadsheet, logged out of his PC and went in search of Plunkett.

A few minutes later he was seated in front of his boss.

"Did you manage to do anything about this Henderson business, sir?"

"I did. I've been speaking to quite a few people about it, as it happens. I'm sorry, Mick, but we have to let it go. I can't give you chapter and verse, but it's come down from the highest level. We have to let the Brits handle it."

"Do you mean the minister?"

"Ach, no. What do they know about anything? No, no, it was a contact I have in our own security services. Our man spoke to their man, and so on. But I have been assured that Henderson didn't murder anyone, and I believe them."

"Maureen will go mad. She hates to let any of these scumbags slip through her fingers. And herself and Sinéad are really good mates. Plus, it doesn't take us any nearer to finding the killer. This is not a good day, boss."

"Maybe you could think of something we could do for Loughran. She's a bonnie girl, and I know she works hard. I'm sure you'll think of something, Mick. Now, can we draw a line under it?"

"Yes, OK, sir. I'll get Maureen to sort something out for Sinéad. What sort of budget have you in mind, sir?"

"Now Mick, you're the man for the budgets. I'm sure you'll find an expense heading to bury it nice and deep, but don't be mean."

"Thanks, sir."

Mick left the Superintendent's office. He had already figured that he could put a gratuity for Sinéad Loughran down to 'repairs', which was in a way, accurate.

Hays called Maureen Lyons to bring her up to date with the conversation earlier with Plunkett.

"I'm fast coming to the view that although Henderson was a bastard, he didn't actually kill Dunne," Lyons said. "I agree with the boss."

"Have you another suspect?"

"Maybe. But I need some actual evidence. I'm working on it, have no fear."

"Good. Now, better news. Plunkett wants us to give Sinéad a few bob for her adventures. He's left it to me to sort it out. Any ideas?" Hays said.

"We could get her one of those prepaid Mastercards. There's a place out on the Ballybrit Industrial Estate that does them. I think that way, she avoids having to pay tax on it."

"Sounds good," Hays said.

"How much are we talking?"

"Let's go a thousand euro. Get them to send the bill for my attention and I'll cover it."

"That's very generous, Mick. Thanks. That will make her arm feel better, for sure. I'll be back later. Oh, and by the way, you may get another call from Arbuthnot. I'm sending one of Séan's men to get his fingerprints. Can you deal with that for me?"

"Can a fish swim? See you later."

Chapter Thirty-five

Jim Dolan had received detailed instructions from Sergeant Mulholland. He walked down through the town as far as the festival offices, climbed the stairs, knocked, and went in.

There was a local girl that Dolan recognised packing away papers into storage boxes and arranging them on a shelving unit.

"Hello, Maeve. I bet you're glad the festival is over. Are you still busy?"

"Oh, hello, Jim. God, don't talk to me. It never stops. What are you doing here anyway?"

"Ah, you know. This murder that happened down at the showgrounds. We're not really getting anywhere with it, so the big cheeses have decided we need to fingerprint the whole damn town. It's a bit of a chore, to be honest, but it has to be done. Were you down at the showgrounds at all during the festival?"

"Yes, of course. Will you be wanting mine then?" Maeve said.

"Yes, I'm afraid so. But I have one of these new-fangled things that does it electronically. It only takes a minute, and there's no messy ink or anything. Do you mind?"

"Nah, you're grand. Just show me what to do."

Dolan used the hand-held device to input the girl's name, and then led her through the procedure as she placed each finger in turn down on the little glass screen.

"And now just your thumb, please."

"I suppose I'm on record now for all time," Maeve said as she finished the process.

"I'm not sure. I just take them; I don't know what happens to them after. Is Mr Arbuthnot in?"

"Yes, he's in his office."

"Could you tell him I'm here, Maeve. I need to get his fingerprints too."

Maeve gave Dolan a withering look. But she went to a solid brown door at the other side of the reception area and knocked. She opened the door, and spoke to the man within. She then withdrew from the room and signalled Jim Dolan to go into Arbuthnot's office.

Dolan explained the purpose of his visit while Arbuthnot sat stoically behind his desk.

"You are joking, Guard. What on earth do you think I could have had to do with anything like that? It's preposterous. I won't have it."

"I'm afraid I will have to insist, sir. I have orders from on high. I can't go back without completing what I came for," Dolan exclaimed.

"Well, that's not my problem. Now can you leave please? I have work to do."

Dolan sat where he was and said nothing.

"Very well. Stay there while I call your superintendent. You haven't heard the last of this, young man," Arbuthnot said solemnly.

Arbuthnot looked up the number he had been given previously for Superintendent Hays. He lifted his phone and dialled.

"Superintendent Hays. This is Mathew Arbuthnot from the Clifden Arts Festival office. I have one of your chaps here who wants to take my fingerprints. What's this all about?"

"Good day, Mr Arbuthnot. As I'm sure the officer explained, we are collecting fingerprints from as many people as we can who attended the festival. It's purely for the purposes of elimination, nothing to worry about."

"You can't seriously believe that I had anything to do with that man's death, can you? It's ridiculous."

"As I said, Mr Arbuthnot, it's purely a procedural matter. You could have had it finished in the time it has taken you to call me. There's no ink involved or anything and it only takes a minute," Hays said.

"It's the principle of the thing, Superintendent. I don't appreciate being treated like a criminal."

"That's not the issue, Mr Arbuthnot. But I'd hate to have to report that you were obstructing our enquiries."

Arbuthnot remained silent for quite a few seconds.

"Very well, Superintendent, but I'm not happy about this. I intend to make my feelings known to your superiors."

"That's your prerogative, of course. But I would appreciate if you could just co-operate with my officer there today," Hays said.

Arbuthnot hung up without another word. He reluctantly offered his fingers one by one to Dolan. Dolan completed the task with his little electronic device in an icy silence, thanked the man for his co-operation, and left. By the time he had got back to the Garda station, the unit had transmitted Arbuthnot's fingerprints to the Garda central control.

When Dolan reappeared in the Clifden Garda station and told Sergeant Mulholland that he had recorded Arbuthnot's fingerprints, Mulholland wasted no time in telling Lyons.

"Arbuthnot's fingerprints are now in the system."

"That's great, Séan. How was your man, anyway?"

"Jim says he was as cranky as a bull with a hangover. He even called your Mick to try and weasel out of it. But it's done now. Let's see what develops."

"Of course, thanks, Séan, and thank Jim for me too. I'll head back to Galway now. Thanks again for your help."

Once she was back on the road, she called Sinéad Loughran.

"Hi, Sinéad. I've just been speaking to Clifden. We have Mathew Arbuthnot's fingerprints in the system now. Will you see if there's a match to the fire extinguisher?"

"Yes, I'll do it right away. Everything else OK, Maureen?" Loughran said, detecting a rather sombre tone from the other end of the line.

"Ah, ye know. I'll be happier if we can move this thing along. Get back to me, won't you?" Lyons said.

"Yes, of course. It will only take me about half an hour. Talk soon."

An hour later, Lyons was back at her desk.

She went back to her thoughts, trying to make the connections in her mind with the information they had collected. It wasn't much, she had to admit. She was deep in speculation when Mick Hays appeared at her door.

"Hi, Mick. Come in."

"Thanks. Are you OK? You look a bit glum."

"Better now," she said smiling, "what can I do for you?"

"It's nothing really. I just wanted to let you know that I had Arbuthnot on the blower when Jim Dolan was getting his fingerprints. He was furious. We'll have to tread very carefully there. Has anything further come to light to connect him with anything?" Hays said.

"Fat chance. Nothing. But Sinéad is working on his prints now. We'll know soon if he handled that fire extinguisher."

"Even if he did, Maureen, it's not at all conclusive. He could make up a whole rake of stories as to why he handled that thing at some stage. It certainly wouldn't prove that he had anything to do with the killing of Adam Dunne. I know you don't like the man, but that doesn't mean he's guilty of murder."

"I know, Mick, but he's an arrogant prick."

"Listen, hun, if you had to lock up all the men in Ireland because they were arrogant pricks, there would be no one left on the streets. But, please, go carefully."

"Yes, sir, Superintendent, sir," Lyons said without a smile.

"Don't be like that, Maureen. Look, I'll try to help if I can. Just don't 'Maureen' the man. Not yet in any case."

"I'm sorry, Mick, it's just…"

"I know, love, I know. But remember softly softly catchy monkey. I'll see you later."

Back in his own office, Hays went through his notebook and dialled a UK number. The phone rang for three rings, and then was answered by a simple, "Yes."

"Hello, Roger. It's Mick Hays here from Ireland."

The man at the other end said nothing, so Hays continued.

"I wonder if you could do something for me? I'd like to know if you have anything on a Mathew Arbuthnot. He's retired now, and lives in Clifden, but I think he may be English."

Watkins said nothing, and after a few moments, the line went dead.

"Jesus! As if eight hundred years wasn't enough!" Hays said to the instrument.

Chapter Thirty-six

"Hi, Maureen. It's Sinéad. Can I pop over for a few minutes?" Loughran said cheerfully when Lyons answered the phone.

"Sure. And bring some coffee for heaven's sake. I need a caffeine boost!"

Ten minutes later, Loughran appeared at Lyons' door carrying a small cardboard tray with two steaming take-away coffees, and a bag with two donuts inside.

"Thanks, Sinéad. You'll go far in this outfit!"

Lyons put two brown sugars into her coffee and started to munch on the donut, trying not to spill jam on her white blouse. When she had devoured a few mouthfuls, she turned her attention to Loughran. "So, what have you got?"

"Well. We did find a fingerprint from Arbuthnot on the can, or should I say a thumbprint."

"Yesss," Lyons said, making a fist of her hand and shaking it in the air.

"But hold on, that's not the full story," Loughran said.

"Why do I know I'm not going to like this?"

"The print is actually a thumbprint, and it's on the base of the can, not the sides. It's not the way he would have been holding it if he was pressing it to Dunne's mouth to asphyxiate him."

"Damn! And is there anything else on the can?"

"A few smudges, but nothing that's any use."

"Bloody hell, Sinéad. I thought we had him," Lyons said.

"Are you sure he did it, Maureen? There's very little evidence."

"I just have a feeling, Sinéad. And even if he didn't do it, he's done something for sure. But I agree. We need more – much more. Is there any point in going back out for another look at the scene?"

"I don't think so. We gave it a very thorough going over last time. I'm sorry."

They finished their refreshments and snacks in silence. Loughran tidied away the wrappings and empty cups, and went to leave.

"I'm sorry it wasn't better news, Maureen. I'd better get back."

"OK, Sinéad. Thanks for the coffee anyway. It's not your fault."

* * *

An hour after Hays' rather odd call with the man from MI5, while he was sitting at his desk reading a report, his PC pinged. An email had arrived. Before opening it, Hays tried to decipher where it had come from. It could after all be one of a dozen or so spam emails that managed to penetrate his email protection software every day. The sender was just a number followed by '@hotmail.com' and the subject line was blank. The email itself was empty, but there was a PDF file attached to it.

Initially, Hays was reluctant to read it, believing that it could contain malware, so he powered up the specialist software he had put on the machine himself and did a deep scan of the document before opening it. It came back clean.

He opened the file which related to Mathew Edgar Arbuthnot. There were twenty-two pages all about the subject, spanning his birth some fifty-five years earlier in South Africa, right through his early years; on into his career as a dealer in precious metals in the UK, to his retirement in Ireland six years previously. Hays didn't study the text in great detail, but he could see that it was a very comprehensive document.

"Maybe Roger Watkins isn't so bad after all."

He sent the file to the printer, and the device clicked and whirred slowly through it, spewing out page after page of densely packed information. When all twenty-two pages had been reproduced, Hays went back to his PC. The file, and the email wrapped around it had both disappeared. He searched in his 'bin' folder; his 'spam' folder and his 'junk' folder on the email client he was using, but there was no sign of any of it. It had simply vanished without trace.

* * *

When Loughran had left, Lyons went out into the open plan and gathered Eamon Flynn and Sally Fahy around her.

"Right, folks. I want us to spend the rest of the day doing a deep dive on one Mathew Arbuthnot. I want everything we can get on him. Banking; revenue records; any interaction with social welfare; local property tax, if any; phone records for the last three months; parking tickets; TV license, and any connection, no matter how tenuous, with Vincent Henderson. By close of play tonight, I want us to know more about Arbuthnot than he knows himself. Got it?"

"Yes, boss," they said in unison.

"Would it be OK to get John O'Connor involved, boss?" Fahy said.

"Yes, of course, and anyone else you can get help from too. I'm not messing about here."

Fahy and Flynn recognised the mood Maureen Lyons was in, so they got busy immediately and worked on through lunch with just a sandwich at their desk for sustenance. Lyons went back to her office still feeling frustrated, but happy that she had at least set something in motion.

She called Séan Mulholland.

"Hi, Séan, it's Maureen. Listen, can I ask you what you know of Mathew Arbuthnot?"

"In what way, Maureen?"

"What does he do with his time, apart from the arts festival, I mean?"

"Let's see now. Well, I think he's on the tidy towns committee. They're mostly active in the spring getting the place spruced up for the judging in high summer. And he might be involved with some of the rest of the town council too, but I'm not sure about that. He travels a bit, as far as I know, as well."

"What does he drive, Séan?"

"Some kind of massive jeep, I think. A silver one."

"Do you have the registration number?"

"No, but I can find it handy enough. Do you want me to get it for you?"

"Yes, please. And as soon as you like, Séan."

"Right. I'll see to it immediately."

Lyons was at this stage unaware of the mysterious file that Mick Hays had received. But it wouldn't be long before he shared it with her.

Chapter Thirty-seven

Hays popped his head around Lyons' office door.

"Hi. Look what I've got," he said. He waved the manilla folder into which he had placed the printout in the air.

"What's that?" Lyons said. She wasn't overly impressed yet. Manilla folders didn't excite her.

"All you ever wanted to know about Mathew Edgar Arbuthnot, but were afraid to ask," he said, coming further into the room.

"Are you serious? Where the hell did you get that?" she said, now greatly cheered up.

"Our man in MI5, but don't tell anyone. He didn't send it. We've never seen it, and it doesn't exist. OK?"

"Whatever! Give it here. Oh, and well done you."

Hays brought a chair around to the same side of the desk as Lyons and placed the file down. They started looking through it together.

"Hmm..." Lyons said as she read. "Precious metals. Cripes, I never realized there even was something called palladium or rhodium. Hang on a sec, I'll just ask Mr Google about them."

Lyons discovered that these elements were used largely in industrial applications, including catalytic converters for cars and for some aircraft parts.

"Most of these are mined in South Africa, and of course we know what else comes from there," Lyons said.

"Yes, we do. Hang on a sec. There's a couple of pages here about some of his travel. Looks like he's been to South Africa several times, but he's also been to the Middle East. Syria."

"Blimey, Mick. Do you think Arbuthnot is one of theirs?"

"Who knows. If he is, he must have done something despicable, like insulted the Queen or something, if they are willing to throw him under the bus."

"Do you think we could honey trap him? It's worked well before."

"No, I don't. We were lucky with Henderson. If he hadn't gone rogue he could easily have pleaded entrapment, and he'd have got off scot-free. No. We'll need different tactics for this charmer. You know what I'm going to say, don't you?"

"'Follow the money', I imagine. It's what you usually say."

"Exactly. I'd say Mr Arbuthnot is sitting on a right pile of ill-gotten gains, and I doubt very much if he's paid all his taxes," Hays said.

"Is there anything in there about overseas bank accounts?" Lyons said, pointing to the open folder.

"I haven't found anything. But wouldn't it be more likely that he's keeping his money in diamonds, or gold rather than currency?"

"I guess you're right. So how do we flush him out? Remember, it's not just a bit of tax dodging we want him for. He could well have seen Adam Dunne off too, if Dunne was getting close to exposing him."

"You're right. Listen, you're much better at this sort of thing than I am. Why don't I leave it with you for a few hours. I'm sure you'll come up with something. But for God's sake, don't let this file out of your sight. If it gets out that MI5 sent it to us, the whole thing could blow up in our faces. We'd both be directing traffic in Ringaskiddy for the rest of our time in the Gardaí."

Lyons smiled, but even as he spoke, the kernel of a plan was forming in her mind.

* * *

"What do you think?" Lyons said to Sally Fahy as she outlined her plan to the young detective sergeant.

"Do you not think it would be better if Eamon went with you, boss? I know it's sexist, but some people respond better to a male."

"I know what you mean, Sally," Lyons said. "But Arbuthnot doesn't like women. We can turn that to our advantage when we are questioning him. I intend to rattle Mathew Edgar Arbuthnot till his teeth come loose. Then we will see what he does next. Simples. Anyway, Eamon will be part of the team watching him after we've finished with him, along with a few of Séan's men."

"Crikey. I almost feel sorry for the poor bloke. Right. You're on. When?"

"I have a feeling Arbuthnot is an early riser. Let's be at his work premises when it opens tomorrow morning. I'll brief Séan in the meantime. I want to lift him in front of his assistant, and make a bit of a show of it out on the street too. That should bring him down a peg or two."

"May I say something, boss?" Fahy asked.

"Yes, of course."

"That's brilliant, but almost evil. You're amazing."

"It's been said before, but don't spread it around. Anyway, you don't get anywhere in this business by being Miss Nice. Remember when you pointed your gun at the thief in the jeweller's shop that time? You were fearless. That's what gets results. I'll pick you up here at, say, seven-thirty tomorrow. OK?"

"Yes, fine."

"Now, scoot. I have some arrangements to make."

When Fahy had left, Lyons took the file that Hays had left behind and put it in the bottom drawer of her filing cabinet beside several others of the same appearance. She then locked the unit and placed the key in her usual hiding place. Then she called Séan Mulholland.

"Are you sure about this, Maureen," he said when she had outlined her plan to the sergeant. "Yer man can be very prickly."

"Yes, Séan, I'm sure. It's the only way."

"And would you not prefer to take him back into the city for questioning?" Mulholland would much prefer if he could put some distance between him and the inevitable unpleasantness that was bound to follow Lyons' tactics.

"No, Séan, I want to do it out there. Firstly, I want it to be visible to the people of the town for maximum humiliation. Secondly, when he reaches for a lawyer, which he will do, it will take whoever he calls ages to get to Clifden, and we'll be keeping Arbuthnot in your holding cell while he waits. Make sure it's nice and chilly."

"Maureen Lyons, you're a wicked woman. But I see what you mean, I hope it doesn't backfire on you. Is Superintendent Hays in the loop?"

"You let me take care of that, Séan. Now, who have we got from your squad for the follow-up operation?"

"I can get Jim and Peadar lined up, and if you need more, I could call on Pascal Brosnan and Mary Fallon from Roundstone. What do you think?"

"Sounds good. Everyone is to be in plain clothes. Jim and Peadar can be on foot close to his office, and we'll make the two from Roundstone the mobile units. They'll need two separate unmarked cars. Sally and I will be on hand too, though in the background as he will have already seen us and we don't want to alert him to what's going on. Have you got enough decent radios to equip the whole team?"

"Yes, I have six almost new ones here. I'll make sure they are charged up. What time will you be here in the morning, Maureen?"

"We plan to call on Arbuthnot's office as soon as it opens."

"That's about nine-thirty, but better be here at nine just in case he comes in early."

"Right. Thanks, Séan. See you in the morning."

Chapter Thirty-eight

The following morning was quite misty in Galway, as was common in autumn. But the forecast predicted that the mist would clear by around half past ten, and then it would be sunny for a few hours before a weather front moved in from the west bringing heavy rain off the Atlantic Ocean.

Lyons met with her colleague at Mill Street at half past seven as arranged, and the two travelled out in convoy; Lyons in her Volvo, and Fahy in her much smaller vehicle. As they passed Maam Cross the sun broke through the morning mist, and they passed the rest of the journey admiring the beautiful scenery that surrounded them while keeping up a steady pace.

They parked the cars, facing in opposite directions, on the street outside Arbuthnot's offices. Fahy got out and joined Lyons in the Volvo.

"We're kind of early. What do we do now?" Fahy said.

"I don't suppose we could get a coffee anywhere at this hour," Lyons said.

"Let me go exploring. I'm sure I'll find something. Do you need a snack too?"

"No. Just a nice strong Americano if you can find it. Thanks."

Fahy walked down to where Market Street and Main Street connected, and was pleased to see that the large supermarket was opening up. She went in, and established that the coffee machine was up to temperature, and purchased two takeaway Americanos in paper cups.

"Well done you," Lyons said, as her colleague juggled with the door of the car and the little cardboard tray holding the hot drinks. She sat in, and both women enjoyed the reviving drink.

At ten past nine, Lyons called Séan Mulholland on his mobile phone.

"Good morning, Maureen. Where are you?"

"We're just outside his office here in the town. Is everything set up?"

"Yes. I have Pascal and Mary on their way in to us in separate cars, and out of uniform as you requested. Jim will be along soon, and Peadar is here already checking out the radios."

"Great. Sally and I will collect ours when we bring Arbuthnot in. I don't suppose you know who his solicitor is, Séan?"

"Haven't a clue. Probably some smart arse from Galway, or maybe even Dublin."

"Excellent. Dublin would be better. He'll be left to stew for hours while whoever it is gets here. OK. See you in a while."

As they drained the last of their coffee, a sleek and quite new, black BMW pulled in a little way up the street. Arbuthnot got out of it, and went to the door of his office, locking the car with a remote fob on his way. They left him to open up properly for ten minutes, then Lyons looked at her colleague. "Right, let's go."

They climbed the stairs leading to the festival offices and entered the outer room. The inner door to Arbuthnot's private office was open. Lyons knocked on the door frame and went straight in.

"Who the hell let you in?" the man said very crossly.

"Good morning, Mr Arbuthnot. This is Detective Sergeant Sally Fahy, a colleague of mine. We'd like you to accompany us to the Garda station here in the town. We need to ask you some questions."

"That's out of the question. I have a meeting with the council at ten-thirty, and I have some papers to prepare before that."

Lyons looked at Fahy and nodded slightly.

"I'm afraid it's not optional, Mr Arbuthnot," Fahy said. She advanced further into the room.

"I've told you. It's not convenient. Now please leave, I have work to do."

"Mr Arbuthnot, I'd prefer not to have to arrest you. But if you won't accompany us willingly, that's exactly what I will do. Of course, that will mean a marked squad car outside here with blue flashing lights, and I'll have to place you in handcuffs."

Arbuthnot stared coldly at Lyons for quite a long time. His stare was returned equally coldly by Lyons who didn't even blink.

"Very well. I'll come along. But I want a solicitor present, and I want to contact that Hays character too and lodge a complaint."

"You may have one call to your solicitor, Mr Arbuthnot. Now, may I have your mobile phone please?" Lyons said, holding out her hand.

The man reluctantly handed over his phone.

"Don't go snooping in that. It's none of your business."

Lyons and Fahy said nothing. They escorted Arbuthnot down to the street where he made a fuss about locking the door to the premises securely, and then he sat into the back of Lyon's Volvo with Fahy for company.

"What's all this about, anyway?" he said as Lyons started the car.

"I'd prefer to wait until we're at the station to start our conversation," she said. The rest of the short journey took place in an icy silence.

Fahy showed Arbuthnot to the station's one and only interview room. It was pretty basic – just a table with a dusty green inlay on its top, and four plastic chairs around it. A single incandescent bulb in an old enamel shade was suspended over the table, and was the room's only source of light.

Fahy asked Arbuthnot for the name and phone number of his solicitor so that he or she could be summoned.

"Don't bother. It will take him too long to get here anyway. Let's just get on with it."

Fahy relayed the information to Lyons who was sitting with Séan Mulholland chatting.

"That's a bit surprising, Sally. But, OK, if that's the way he wants it, let's make a start."

* * *

"Mr Arbuthnot, as you know we are investigating the murder of Adam Dunne that took place at the showgrounds during the arts festival. As you told us previously, you are in charge of all that goes on there. What can you tell us about this matter?" Lyons said.

"Is this what all this is about? You could have asked me about this up at my office. No need for all the drama."

"Could you just answer my question please?"

"Absolutely nothing," Arbuthnot said and folded his arms defiantly.

"Was Mr Dunne an exhibitor at the festival?" Lyons said.

"I'd have to check our records which are back at the office, but I don't think so. I think he must have just been a visitor."

"So how come he was in the marquee after the place had closed for the night then?"

"How should I know? Maybe he got locked in by accident. Anyway, it's Gifford you should be asking about that. He was in charge of securing the place."

"But if he just got locked in by accident as you say, that's hardly a reason to murder him now, is it?" Lyons said.

Arbuthnot just snorted.

Lyons tapped her colleague's foot under the table.

"What do you know about diamonds, Mr Arbuthnot?" Fahy asked.

"Very little. Precious metals are my thing. You know, titanium, platinum, even gold."

"Have you ever traded in diamonds at all?" Fahy pressed on.

Arbuthnot became a little more animated at the question.

"No, never. Now when can I get out of here? I've answered all your questions."

"Where do you live, Mr Arbuthnot?"

"You know very well where I live. I have a house out on the Doonen Road about a mile outside town."

"Would you have any objection to us having a look around your house?" Lyons said.

"Yes, I bloody would. Look, what's all this about? There's clearly something going on you're not telling me about. I have a right to know."

"You're right, Mr Arbuthnot, there is. You see information has come to our attention that Mr Dunne was in some way connected with diamond smuggling. We only have the scantiest detail for now, but it's a line of enquiry that we are keen to follow up. Have you ever heard of blood diamonds?" Lyons said.

"Isn't that where diamonds are used to fund terrorism or something? I think I may have read about it somewhere."

"Yes, exactly. I know it sounds very far-fetched, and why anyone in Ireland would be involved is beyond us, for now, but we've only just started digging, if you'll excuse the pun."

"Well, I'm afraid I can't help you there. And as you say yourself, it seems highly implausible that there could be any connection to Ireland, let alone the Clifden Arts Festival."

"So, when can we come and have a look around your property, Mr Arbuthnot?" Fahy said.

"When you have a warrant, Inspector, and not before."

"Very well. Please remain here for the moment. I'll just go and set the wheels in motion."

"You can't keep me here. I'm a busy man. It's not right."

"Neither is murder, Mr Arbuthnot."

Lyons and Fahy got up and left the room.

Back in the office to the rear of the public area in the Garda station, Fahy turned to Lyons. "What now, boss?"

"Leave him sweat where he is for an hour or so. Then you go down and tell him he can go. Don't say anything else to him. Just that. Then we'll see what he does next."

Chapter Thirty-nine

After an hour with very little happening, Fahy went back to the interview room and told Arbuthnot he was free to leave.

"What? Is that it?" he said.

"Yes," Fahy said coolly, "we may need to talk to you again, but that's all for now."

"What a bloody waste of my time. You haven't heard the end of this, young lady. Not by a long chalk."

Arbuthnot stomped out of the room, up the stairs and out the door, moving rather more quickly than his proclaimed innocence would suggest.

When he was walking back up to his office, Lyons activated the surveillance team. Each of the group had a radio and a unique call signal. Lyons was Alpha One, Fahy Alpha Two and so on. They observed Arbuthnot discreetly as he approached his office, but he didn't go in. Instead, he went straight to his car, sat in and drove off.

"Right, Sally, follow him, but for God's sake don't get seen. Report in as soon as you can determine where he is headed."

"OK, boss."

Arbuthnot drove down through the town and onto the R341 as if he was going for Ballyconneely. But once he had crossed the Owenglin River, he turned off onto Doonen Road.

"Alpha Two to Alpha One. He's turned onto the Doonen Road."

"Thanks," Lyons said.

"Peadar, can you get out onto the N59 and turn down Doonen Road from the far end. Stay out of sight, but we need to be able to follow him if he takes off in that direction."

"Right, boss. I'm on it."

Arbuthnot drove on down the narrow road for almost a kilometre till he arrived at a beautiful modern house overlooking a large expanse of water known as the Salt Lake. The house was a double-fronted dormer bungalow, faced in Galway stone, with a long, curved tarmac driveway leading up to the slightly elevated property which had magnificent views out to sea.

Fahy found a hidden gateway that led into a disused farmyard a little way back and drove into it. She was close to Arbuthnot's property, but was fairly sure she hadn't been seen as he was too busy navigating the entrance to his house, which was guarded by electric metal gates, to see behind him.

"Alpha Two to Alpha One. He's turned into a big house here at the Salt Lake. I think it's his residence. What do you want me to do?"

"Send the co-ordinates to Alpha Three and see if you can observe what he is doing. Out."

When she had alerted Tobin, Fahy turned her car so that it was pointed towards the entrance to the old yard, ready for a quick getaway, if needed. She positioned it behind the stone wall that marked the perimeter of the yard, so that it couldn't be seen from the road. She got out, and crossing the marshy field while staying bent low, she scrambled her way to the edge of Arbuthnot's neatly tended garden. From her elevated position, she could see Arbuthnot moving around inside. He was clearly in a hurry, and from what Fahy could see, he was packing a large black bag with clothes and other stuff from his bedroom. After a few minutes, he took a final look around and left the house, getting back into his BMW and setting forth.

Fahy crept back across the field towards her car while reporting in on the radio.

"He's on the move."

"Which way is he going?"

"Hang on. He's turned back towards Clifden, boss."

"OK. Don't follow him. It's too risky. I'll get Jim to pick him up as Doonen Road joins the R341. You hang back and await further instructions."

"OK."

Lyons relayed the information to Dolan via the radio and told him to wait at the junction for Arbuthnot's BMW and then follow him discreetly.

Arbuthnot drove up along Market Street and then turned onto Seaview with Jim Dolan following at a safe distance. He then joined the Sky Road, and continued in a westerly direction. Dolan radioed in.

"Heading west on the Sky Road towards Kingstown. Subject still in sight."

Lyons put the fourth member of her surveillance team into action.

"Pascal, can you go out on the Westport Road as quick as you can. Turn in at the caravan park and scoot across to the Sky Road on the old track. Position yourself at the far junction of the Lower Sky Road and the main Sky Road and stay out of sight. Go as quickly as you can, and await further instructions."

"Right, Inspector. Will I take Mary with me?"

"Yes, but hurry."

Lyons radio crackled into life again.

"Subject has turned down onto the Lower Sky Road. He's moving quickly, but I still have eyes on him."

"OK. Keep in touch."

"Where do you think he's off to?" Séan Mulholland said in a lull between radio calls.

"I think I might have an idea, Séan, but let's wait and see."

They didn't have long to wait.

"Subject has turned into the lane beside the old coastguard station," said Dolan, over the radio.

"I thought that might be where he was going," said Lyons. "OK, Jim. When he's out of the car, park yours across the entrance so he can't leave. I'll get the troops moving in your direction."

Then she barked into her radio, "All units. Head for the old coastguard station on the Lower Sky Road. Quick as you can. I'm on my way too."

* * *

It didn't take long for Lyons to get to the site. She pressed the Volvo as hard as she dared, and it responded by whisking her along at pace to the old coastguard station. When she got there, Jim Dolan was sitting in his car parked across the laneway leading up to the abandoned yard, and Sally Fahy had just arrived and was parking at the other side of the road. When Lyons arrived, they all got out.

"OK, everyone. I presume chummy is still up there?"

"Yes, boss," Dolan said, "unless he's taken off on foot across the bog."

Lyons gave Jim Dolan a withering look.

"Right. You stay here, Jim. You're the backstop. Sally, with me."

The two women walked up along the narrow lane. This time, they didn't care if they were seen. It would make no difference to the inevitable outcome. When they got to the yard, Lyons turned to her colleague. "Have a look in the car, Sally. See what's in his big black bag."

Lyons went on into the old shed where she saw Arbuthnot working on a statuette on the bench. When he heard her approach, he turned around.

"God! Not you again! Have you been following me? This is harassment. I'll have your badge for this."

Lyons was unperturbed.

"What are you doing?" she said.

"None of your business. Now get out of here before I lose my temper." He reached behind him and lifted a hammer from the bench and started towards Lyons.

Lyons was quick. She reached to her belt and released her telescopic metal truncheon, flicked it so that it extended to its full length, and with one sweeping movement brought it down heavily on Arbuthnot's arms.

He dropped the hammer and yelped. "You bitch! You've broken my bloody arm!"

"Mr Arbuthnot," Lyons responded, "I'm arresting you–"

"Hold on, boss." It was Sally Fahy who had just come into the shed carrying a black cardboard box about twelve centimetres square. "You might like to see this."

Lyons looked at the item Fahy was carrying.

"Cuff him," she said. "Hands in front, I think I may have broken his arm."

Fahy gave Lyons the box which she opened carefully. Inside there was a sponge square which she lifted to reveal what must have been nearly a hundred diamonds of various sizes sparkling brightly in the dim light inside the shed.

Lyons replaced the lid on the box.

"Mathew Arbuthnot, I'm arresting you for assaulting a police officer; being in possession of contraband; and for the murder of Adam Dunne. You do not have to say anything…"

Chapter Forty

This time, Arbuthnot had equipped himself with a solicitor. While they were waiting for the man to arrive, Arbuthnot had been taken to the local hospital and was informed that his arm was not in fact broken, merely bruised. He was discharged after a few minutes.

Dylan Keaveney from the firm of the same name had arrived out from Galway, and had been given thirty minutes to confer with his client before Lyons and Fahy started the interview. Flynn was on standby to take over, if required.

"Now, really, Inspector, what's all this nonsense about my client attacking you? He was simply startled by your sudden appearance at his workbench, as anyone would have been. He didn't mean you any harm," Keaveney said in an oily voice.

"So, when he came at me shouting with a hammer in his hand raised to shoulder height, he was just being friendly, was he? And don't forget, I have a witness. Another service officer who saw the whole thing. Let's cut the nonsense, to use your word, Mr Keaveney."

She turned to Arbuthnot.

"Mr Arbuthnot, as you know we found a box containing a number of diamonds in a bag in your car. The same bag that you had been observed packing at your home some time earlier in the day. Do you have KP certificates and VAT receipts for those?"

"No comment," Arbuthnot replied.

"My client," Keaveney said, "is, as you know, involved in the precious metals trade. He–"

"I thought he was retired?" Lyons interrupted.

"If you'd just let me finish, Inspector. Mr Arbuthnot is, or was, involved in precious metals. Much of that as you may be aware is mined in South Africa. Occasionally, when these metals are extracted, some precious stones are found as well. Mr Arbuthnot came across such a find, and purchased the stones along with several tons of metal ore for resale. It's all perfectly legitimate, Inspector."

"So, he will have all that documentation supporting what you have said readily available then. Where is it?" Lyons said.

"Unfortunately, when Mr Arbuthnot moved from the UK to Ireland, several boxes of his paperwork were mislaid by the carrier. Among those boxes was the paperwork you are looking for, so I'm afraid it's gone."

"How very convenient. But that doesn't get you off the hook, Mr Arbuthnot. Since the UK left the EU, VAT would be due to the Irish Revenue on importation of your hoard. What's it all worth, in round numbers?"

Arbuthnot didn't meet her eyes. "No comment."

"Well, I'm no expert," Lyons continued, "but let's say a quarter of a million. VAT, at twenty-three per cent, would be, let's see, sixty thousand or thereabouts. And that's just for this lot. Our people are out at your workshop just now, and I'd wager they'll find a good few more diamonds concealed in those hideous statues you are so fond of."

Lyons let her message sink in.

"But to be really honest, Mr Arbuthnot," she said, "I don't give a cat's curse about the diamonds. Our Criminal

Assets Bureau can take care of all that. In case you're not aware, they confiscate this kind of stuff all the time, and then it's up to you to prove that you came by it legitimately, all tax paid and all. So, good luck with that. No. I'm much more interested in the death of Adam Dunne. You previously told me you knew nothing of that matter, and didn't know the man either, is that right?"

"Yes, I already told you this," Arbuthnot said.

Lyons opened the manilla folder she had brought with her into the room, and took out a photograph.

"I'm showing Mr Arbuthnot a still image taken from CCTV recorded at Blue Dolphin Marine in Galway. Would you agree that this is you in the picture, Mr Arbuthnot?"

Arbuthnot leaned forward and studied the photograph.

"Yes, possibly."

Lyons took another photograph from her folder. This one was a close-up shot of the base of the can they had retrieved from the waste disposal at the arts festival.

"I'm showing Mr Arbuthnot a photograph of the base of a fire extinguisher, similar to the one we believe he purchased in Blue Dolphin. That, Mr Arbuthnot, is your fingerprint on the base of the can. The same item that you bought a few days before Dunne was murdered by asphyxiation using this device."

Arbuthnot looked to Keaveney who made no response.

"Why did you kill him?" Lyons said.

"He was a spy," Arbuthnot said.

"And tell me, Mr Arbuthnot, when you purchased the fire extinguisher in Blue Dolphin, was it your intention to use it to kill Adam Dunne?"

"Yes, it was."

Keaveney quickly reached across and put his hand on Arbuthnot's arm. "My client is very distressed, Inspector. He doesn't know what he is saying. I want a break."

"Very well. But before we break for thirty minutes, I'd like your client to confirm that he did in fact kill Adam

Dunne using the fire extinguisher at the showgrounds in Clifden."

Arbuthnot just nodded.

"For the tape, Mr Arbuthnot has nodded in agreement."

Lyons switched off the recording device and the two detectives got up and left the room.

Outside in the corridor, Fahy turned to her boss. "Fantastic, boss. Well done. I thought there for a while he was going to get away with it. Our evidence was pretty circumstantial."

"Ah, yes, but he thought we had more. That's why I went for the diamonds and the assault first. I think he was convinced we had him banged to rights. But he won't be able to worm his way out of a confession, that's for sure. But hold the phone, as they say, I'm not finished yet!"

Thirty minutes later, Fahy and Lyons re-entered the interview room in the basement of Clifden Garda station.

"My client would like to make a statement, Inspector," Keaveney said.

"Very well. But first, I have a few more questions. How did you know Dunne was a spy?"

"He let it slip one day when we were doing a deal on some stones. We were talking about another dealer and he said 'don't touch him, he's with MI5'. The only way he could have known that is if he was MI5 himself."

"And what about Henderson?" Lyons said.

"He was OK. We did a good bit of business with him, but he vanished in a hurry. I don't know what became of him," Arbuthnot said.

Lyons decided not to enlighten the man.

"What about the Syrian connection?"

"That's where the money ends up. We sell the diamonds, mostly in Amsterdam or Antwerp. I take my cut, and the balance is sent electronically around the houses. But I'm fairly certain it ends up in Syria."

"And it doesn't bother you that the money could be used to buy weapons and bombs that kill innocent people?"

"That's not my concern, Inspector. If I didn't handle the stuff, someone else would. That's just the way things are these days," Arbuthnot said.

"Right, well I'll leave Detective Fahy here to take your statement, Mr Arbuthnot. We'll try and get you into court tomorrow, but I imagine you will be remanded for trial."

"Bail?" Keaveney said.

"Unlikely, Mr Keaveney."

Chapter Forty-one

Lyons went back upstairs to where the rest of the team were gathered having a well-earned cup of tea.

"What's the story?" Mulholland asked.

Lyons filled them all in with what had transpired, and broad smiles broke out all around.

"God, that's great, Maureen. Another one bites the dust, as it were," Mulholland said. He extended his hand and shook Lyons' firmly.

"Yes, a good result. But it was a big team effort. Thanks to all of you, and Sinéad, of course. Jim, will you ring her and tell her? I want to give Mick a call."

"Yes, sure."

Lyons got through to her partner straight away. She told him about the confession.

"That's great, Maureen. They don't really stand a chance with you on their case. Is it OK if I call Watkins and let him know? I think we owe him that much."

"Sure, but he's not getting his hands on Arbuthnot. He's ours for the next fifteen years or so anyway. Listen, would you do something for me?"

"Sure."

"Can you get in touch with the CAB? There's probably a few million sloshing around in various bank accounts and heaven knows how many more blood diamonds are out there too. They could have a field day."

"Yes, no problem. I know one of the chiefs over there. I'll give him a call. And to think we were worried about the two we got from Dunne's car that Sinéad was keeping safe for us in her handbag!"

"Cripes, yes. I'd forgotten about that. We should have let her keep them."

"Now, now, Inspector. None of that kind of talk. Remember, I'm still a senior officer."

"Piss off, Mick. Listen, I should be back in later. I'm bloody exhausted. Can we go out for eats tonight? I can't cook."

"Yes, of course. I'll book somewhere nice. Should we bring Sinéad? You know, sort of a celebration," Hays said.

"I think you quite fancy that pretty little blonde forensic scientist, Mick Hays."

"Not a bit of it. But it does my image no harm in the town to be seen out and about with two beautiful women. I'll see if she's free."

"OK. Whatever. Probably a good idea. She did have a rough time with Henderson."

"Right. I'll see you later then. What time will you be back?"

"I should be there by no later than six."

"Great. See you then."

When she had finished the call with Hays, Lyons found Séan Mulholland.

"Séan, I don't think we're quite finished with this thing yet. There may still be a few of those grotty statues in circulation, and some may have contraband diamonds hidden inside. Can you see if you can track them down? I imagine most of them were bought by locals – have them examined."

"Yes, OK. Though if we do find buried treasure, what will happen to it?" Mulholland said.

"It will have to be turned in, of course. And by the way, you'll need to tell whoever runs the thing that they'll need a new boss-man for the festival next year. Arbuthnot won't be available."

"Gosh, you're right. Sure, I might even do the job myself!" he said, laughing.

* * *

The rest of the day went by quickly. Some more officers were brought in to search the shed out by the old coastguard station thoroughly, and then they moved on to Arbuthnot's home. In a filing cabinet in his house, they found a paper trail of money transfers that went literally all around the world, sending very big sums on a circuitous route to whatever faction of terrorists would ultimately benefit.

Back in Galway, Hays was busy.

"Hello, is that Roger Watkins?" he said.

"Yes. Mick. What's up?"

"I just thought I'd let you know we've arrested Mathew Arbuthnot for the murder of Adam Dunne, among other things. I hope he isn't one of yours too?"

"No, definitely not. But we would like the chance to have a little chat with him."

"That could be tricky, Roger. But you've been helpful to us, so I'll see what I can do. Another short break to Ireland for you, maybe?"

"It might not be me this time, but yes, something like that."

"Right, well, leave that with me. I'll be in touch."

"Thanks, Mick."

Hays then called his mate in the Criminal Assets Bureau and put them onto the diamonds, and Mathew Arbuthnot's bank accounts.

"And you're sure, Mick, that none of this is kosher?"

"Positive mate. I'll send you over a few pages from a file I got on him. That'll get you started."

"OK, thanks, Mick. Nice one."

* * *

Lyons, Loughran and Hays met in O'Connaire's restaurant overlooking the docks in Galway city. They ordered from the extensive menu, and Hays asked the two women what wine they would like. After a quick exchange, they settled on a chardonnay, and it was brought to the table by their waitress who gave Lyons a taster to approve.

"Perfect, thanks."

When the waitress had poured a glass for the other two, and topped Lyons' glass up, Hays raised his glass.

"Well, ladies, to you. A great result all round."

The three of them clinked glasses.

"Have you updated Plunkett, Mick?"

"Yes. Poor man doesn't quite know what to do with all the information we've landed him with, but he's pleased that the murder is cleared up anyway. I imagine he'll have some fun dealing with the Brits, but it's all good. The CAB might make a few bob out of it too. I hadn't realized that diamonds can't be detected by airport security. It's no wonder they're used as a sort of currency by the underworld."

"I don't think I want to see another diamond for quite a long time," Loughran said.

"Don't believe a word of it, Mick. If a nice hunky guy came along and swept you off your feet, Sinéad, you'd be back in the diamond business in a flash!" Lyons said.

The three of them laughed out loud.

List of Characters

Detective Superintendent Mick Hays – in overall charge of the detectives at Mill Street Garda station.

Superintendent Finbarr Plunkett – a wily senior officer who tries to keep everyone happy.

Senior Inspector Maureen Lyons – a feisty detective with a strong track record for solving crime in Galway.

Inspector Eamon Flynn – a tenacious detective who follows a line of enquiry to the very end.

Detective Sally Fahy – a pretty young officer who is a lot tougher than she looks.

Sergeant Séan Mulholland – runs the Clifden Garda station with traditional methods, but his experience ensures that he gets results.

Garda Jim Dolan – Séan Mulholland's right-hand man.

DI Willie McNee – a Detective Inspector from Dublin.

Garda Peadar Tobin – another member of the Clifden police team.

Garda Pascal Brosnan – runs the Roundstone Garda station.

Garda Mary Fallon – Pascal Brosnan's helper in Roundstone.

Garda John O'Connor – a nerdy uniformed officer who loves tinkering with technology.

Dr Julian Dodd – an excellent pathologist with a dry sense of humour.

Sinéad Loughran – a good humoured forensic officer.

Keith Buckley – an assistant forensic officer.

Adam Dunne – an antique dealer of sorts with a hidden personality.

Roger Watkins – works with the British security services.

Vincent Henderson – a shady type who doesn't mind getting his hands dirty.

Mathew Arbuthnot – a retired precious metal dealer with an interesting side line.

Charlie Gifford – groundsman at the Clifden showgrounds.

Agnes Feeney – a woman who keeps a guest house.

Clive Richardson – a jeweller.

Dylan Keaveney– a slick solicitor.

Finn Gilpin – a butcher.

If you enjoyed this book, please let others know by leaving a quick review on Amazon. Also, if you spot anything untoward in the paperback, get in touch. We strive for the best quality and appreciate reader feedback.

editor@thebookfolks.com

www.thebookfolks.com

MORE BOOKS BY DAVID PEARSON

In this series:

Murder on the Old Bog Road (Book 1)
Murder at the Old Cottage (Book 2)
Murder on the West Coast (Book 3)
Murder at the Pony Show (Book 4)
Murder on Pay Day (Book 5)
Murder in the Air (Book 6)
Murder at the Holiday Home (Book 7)
Murder on the Peninsula (Book 8)
Murder at the Races (Book 9)
Murder in a Safe Haven (Book 10)
Murder in an Irish Bog (Book 11)
Murder in a Seaside Town (Book 12)
Murder by the Hidden Bay (Book 13)

In the Dublin Homicides Series:

A Deadly Dividend
A Fatal Liaison
The China Chapter
Lethal in Small Doses
Plane Dead
Passion for Murder

If you have enjoyed David Pearson's Galway Homicides series, check out his series of murder mysteries set in Dublin.

Two very different police officers work together to solve cases in this Irish mystery series with a cozy feel.

For Detective Inspector Aidan Burke, policing Dublin's streets is a duty, but protecting his officers comes first. That provides a good environment for promising detectives like DS Fiona Moore to grow. As this series of murder mysteries set in the metropolitan but at times parochial city and its surroundings progresses, we see Moore tackle difficult and dangerous cases with a good success rate. As Burke himself rises in rank, they become a formidable crime fighting duo.

OTHER TITLES OF INTEREST

MURDER ON A YORKSHIRE MOOR by Ric Brady

Ex-detective Henry Ward is settling awkwardly into retirement in a quiet corner of Yorkshire when during a walk on the moor he stumbles upon the body of a young man. Suspecting foul play and somewhat relishing the return to a bit of detective work, he resolves to find out who killed him. But will the local force appreciate him sticking his nose in?

DEAD SET ON MURDER by Iain Henn

Eighteen years after disappearing without a trace, Jennifer's husband's body turns up, yards from her home. Apparently without aging one bit. She knows something is seriously amiss. Fortunately, homicide detective Neil Lachlan shares her concerns. But when the case overlaps with a manhunt for a serial killer, it will put Jennifer's life on the line.

All our books are FREE with Kindle Unlimited and available in paperback.

www.thebookfolks.com

Printed in Great Britain
by Amazon

19890240R00130